MARS
THE
AVENGER

A MYSTERY IN ANCIENT ROME

ALAN SCRIBNER

Torcular Press

Cover: Part of the model of ancient Rome in the Museum of
Roman Civilization in Rome.

ISBN: 1463789785
ISBN-13: 9781463789787
Library of Congress Control Number: 2011913790

CreateSpace, North Charleston, SC

Dedication
Ruth and Paul

TABLE OF CONTENTS

PERSONAE

Marcus Flavius Severus - Judge in the Court of the Urban Prefect

Judge Severus' familia

Artemisia - Severus' wife
Aulus – Severus' 7-year-old son
Flavia – Severus' 5-year-old daughter
Alexander - slave-librarian
Scorpus - slave in charge of the household
Tryphon - slave-valet
Glycon – slave
Argos – family dog
Phaon – family cat

Judge Severus' court staff

Quintus Proculus - court clerk
Caius Vulso - centurion in the Urban Cohort
Publius Aelianus Straton - *tesserarius* in the Urban Cohort
Gaius Sempronius Flaccus - judicial assessor

Lucius Junius Ferox - Roman Senator

Senator Ferox' familia

Fabia - Ferox' wife
Menelaus - slave in charge of the household
Probus - slave in charge of a squad of ten
Harpax - slave in charge of a squad of ten
Tisander - slave in charge of a squad of ten
Phryne - Fabia's *ornatrix*-slave
Timotheus - Greek philosopher

Croesus - former slave in Ferox' *familia*

Anaximander - citizen of Ephesus, a mosaicist

Quintus Lollius Urbicus - Prefect of the City of Rome
(Urbicus is an historical personage and was in fact the
Urban Prefect at the time the story takes place)

Sextus Anicius Metellus — Roman soldier in the Praetorian Guard

Taurus - ex-gladiator and proprietor of a taverna

Squilla - slave dealer

Plotina - Roman matron

The story is set in and around the City of Rome in October of the year 158 CE during the reign of the emperor Antoninus Pius.

The Ides of October fall on October 15.

Times of day: The Roman day was divided into 12 day hours starting from sunrise and 12 night hours from sunset. The length of the hour and the onset time of the hour depended on the season since there is more daylight in summer, more night in winter.

For October, close to an equinox, the hours were approximately equal to our hours in length and the first day hour ran from about 6-7 a.m; the first night hour from 6-7 p.m.

For other times specifically mentioned in the book:

The second day hour – 7-8 a.m.

The third day hour – 8-9 a.m.

The fifth day hour – 10-11 a.m.

The third night hour – 8-9 p.m.

ANCIENT ROME

The pictures on the cover and on the left show part of the model of ancient Rome in the Museum of Roman Civilization in Rome.

The numbers on the picture on the left locate places mentioned in the book, according to the following key:

1. Forum of Augustus with the Temple of Mars the Avenger;
2. Caelian Hill area, where both Judge Severus and Senator Ferox live;
3. Baths of Trajan;
4. Flavian Amphitheater (later called the Colosseum);
5. Road to Ostia and area of Athena's Mantle hotel;
6. Subura area, Taurus' taverna;
7. Slave market;
8. Vicus Tuscus, apartment of Croesus;
9. Street leading to Via Flaminia and Ferox' villa;
10. Circus Maximus

MARCUS FLAVIUS SEVERUS
TO HIMSELF

It is not because it has become fashionable to write meditations "To Oneself" that I am prompted to start my own, but rather because I wish to record the true facts of the case of Anaximander, Fabia and Ferox. Though a sensation in the City, that case was imperfectly understood by those who gossiped so much about it, and the official records, preserved in the Tabularium archives, do not fully divulge its secrets.

Moreover, of all the cases I presided over as a Judge in the Court of the Urban Prefect, this was the only one I wish I had never solved. Like Oedipus, blindly pursuing the knowledge that would destroy him, I thoughtlessly followed the path of logic and deduced the truth. In the end, I confronted horror and irony in the manner of a Roman judge rather than as a Greek philosopher. I therefore refrained from falsifying the records.

The case didn't start luridly for me, as it did for the rest of the City of Rome, with the discovery of Anaximander's mangled body on the steps of the Temple of Mars the Avenger. That occurred five days before the Ides of October in the year 911 After the Founding of the City. Rather it began the day before, when I was summoned to the Prefectura Building by the Urban Prefect — in those days the former general Quintus Lollius Urbicus. The prefect informed me that Fabia, the wife of Senator Lucius Junius Ferox, was missing, and assigned me to find her.

I hardly remember the interview with the prefect. But I distinctly recall discussing the case with my slave Alexander the next day at about the same time Anaximander's body was being carted away from the temple where Rome honors vengeance.

FIVE DAYS BEFORE THE IDES

I

A DISAPPEARANCE

The bronze bird on the water clock chirped the second hour as Marcus Flavius Severus, Judge in the Court of the Urban Prefect in the City of Rome, prepared to leave for work. While he stood erect munching his breakfast of white bread soaked in milk and honey, his slave-valet, Tryphon, meticulously arranged the toga over his master's tunic. Each fold of the snowy white garment was precisely draped to lend an air of ease, elegance and authority to its wearer. A narrow reddish-purple vertical stripe on his tunic was deliberately left uncovered by the toga to display a symbol of Severus' Equestrian class. A plain gold ring and black patrician shoes evinced other symbols of his social status, while the reddish-purple embroidered toga hem announced his judicial authority.

Severus was tall and angular, with slender arms and legs. A slightly hawkish nose and sensual mouth complimented his most noticeable feature - bright, sparkling gray eyes that gave him a look of vitality and intelligence.

The judge wore his hair and beard fashionably short, trimmed and curly, in the style of the emperor. A few wisps of gray, here and there, cropped up amid its full reddish-brown color.

Taking a deep breath, Severus purposely inhaled the clean aroma of freshly washed marble. He was looking forward to the day and felt particularly energetic. The new case, he thought, was just the stimulus he needed after being assigned from the panel of judges to a solid month in court disposing of street crime. The endless stream of frauds, robberies, beatings and killings had been depressing. In criminal court he felt he was on the front line in a war against the lower classes. Order had to be enforced in the City, in "the great sewer" as Juvenal called it, and crime had to be avenged. But it was a judge's duty to impose fines and floggings, exile and hard labor, and various forms of the death penalty against the poor and ignorant, as well as the venal and evil. Though the arbitrary powers of a magistrate allowed Severus some latitude for the exercise of *humanitas*, the task wore him down spiritually because *humanitas* was not necessarily his objective, his intention or his emotion.

Severus impatiently tilted his head so that Tryphon could stick a dressing of oiled spider web to a shaving cut on his cheek, just at the edge of the beard.

"You should keep the spider web on until you reach your office, *domine*," Tryphon advised. "The cut should heal by then. I'll have the razor sharpened again today," he added quickly in response to Severus' glare.

His dress finished, the judge strode briskly into his library, where he knew he would find Alexander, his slave-librarian. A thousand volumes lined the walls, the scrolls arranged horizontally in handsome wooden cubbyholed bookcases, red label tags dangling from their spindled ends. Alexander was seated on a bench carefully mending a scroll. He wore a simple but expensive blue tunic with thin yellow stripes — *clavi* — running from each shoulder down the tunic, shoulder to hem, back and front. A yellow leather thong snaked through his dark hair and a pale blue belt went around his midsection. Alexander had a thin scholarly face and a light, almost ethereal, manner about him. His boyish enthusiasms catered to Severus' sense of playfulness and his deep knowledge of culture fed the judge's wide range of interests. "Others have Pliny in thirty-five volumes," Severus often remarked fondly, "but I have Alexander."

"Did you sleep well, *kyrie?*" the slave inquired politely in Greek.

"About as well as usual," answered the judge in the same language as he crossed the room, "considering that the waterpipes were dripping again from upstairs. For the 10,000 sesterces I pay every year in rent for this so-called luxury apartment," he added sarcastically, "you'd at least expect the plumbing to work." He glanced at the title of the book being repaired. "I have a job for you today, Alexander."

The slave applied some glue and looked up.

"In your acquaintance with literature," asked Severus, "have you ever encountered a story or a reference to a queen and a fisherman?"

Alexander thought a few moments. "Not offhand. Why?"

"Yesterday the Prefect of the City selected me from the panel of judges to investigate a case and something peculiar has been found."

"About a fisherman and a queen?"

"Yes. Let me tell you the problem."

The judge clasped his hands behind his back and began pacing the mosaic floor. "I've been assigned to investigate the disappearance of Fabia, the wife of a retired senator, Lucius Junius Ferox. Ferox, I'm told, had a distinguished career in the army and the government before entering the Senate. But illness forced his retirement two years ago. Ferox and Fabia live in a mansion on the Caelian Hill, just a few streets from here, though for the past week Ferox has been at a country villa north of the City, while Fabia remained in Rome. The Urban Prefect has known them personally for a long time. They were married twenty years ago, when Fabia was fifteen and Ferox thirty-five. It was a marriage of convenience; status for her and for her family, money for him. The prefect described Fabia as very good looking, fashionable and highly social. Ferox, he says, has recently become morose, reclusive and somewhat strange." Severus looked amused. "A perfect pair. In any event, Fabia disappeared the day before yesterday, the seventh day before the Ides. After the lunch siesta, she told the house slaves she was going to the silk market, and with her personal slave Phryne accompanying her, she left the Caelian Hill mansion. Neither of them has returned; not that evening for dinner, nor later that night, nor all day yesterday."

"When did the house slaves first become worried?" asked Alexander.

Severus smiled in appreciation. Fabia's household slaves would know how long to regard any unexplained absence as an escapade.

"They become concerned when she didn't return for dinner, worried when she didn't come back that night, and alarmed when they hadn't heard from her by the next morning. Yesterday morning, an old man named Menelaus, who has been the chief slave of Fabia's household for many years, sent messages around to her friends. No one had seen her. He sent other slaves to scour the shops in the silk market, but the shopkeepers where she usually buys hadn't seen her either. It seemed as if she had vanished, as if some Persian magician had worked a spell over Fabia and her slave Phryne. By yesterday afternoon Menelaus decided to seek help and he reported the matter to the *Vigiles*. Because of the senator's status, the Urban Prefect was quickly informed. He summoned Menelaus, heard the story, and assigned me to look into it."

"What does Senator Ferox have to say about his wife's disappearance?"

"I don't know. As I said, he's away from the City. Besides, the prefect instructed Menelaus not to inform Ferox just yet. He didn't want to alarm the senator unduly. I gather the prefect suspects she ran off with a lover for a few days." He stopped pacing and sat down on the bench next to Alexander. "What I did yesterday was to send my police aides, Vulso and Straton, to Fabia's home to look around and ask some more questions." He reached within the folds of his toga and took out a wooden message-tablet. "Last night," he said, undoing the tablet threads, "Vulso brought this over."

Alexander peered at the waxed page inside. It showed a seal impression of a woman with a crown and a man with a fishing pole. The engraving was somewhat crude, but clearly recognizable as a queen and a fisherman. Alexander studied it with a slightly perplexed look, then handed the tablet back to the judge.

"What does it have to do with Fabia's disappearance?"

"I don't know. Her slaves said she received this tablet shortly before she left the house two days ago. Vulso found it on her dressing table." He stood up. "See what you can find out about a fisherman and a queen. There may be a story behind those symbols."

"Do you think someone went fishing and caught Fabia?"

"I don't know that. What I do know is that I want to find the person who sent it."

Before Alexander could respond, the children Aulus and Flavia rushed into the library, along with the family's large black guard-dog Argos, to say their goodbyes — *salve, vale* — before leaving for school. The children kissed their father while Argos licked his hand. Severus kissed them back, patted their heads and petted Argos, who along with the slave-pedagogue waiting impatiently at the library entrance with school bags and leash, would escort the children to school.

Then Scorpus, the slave in charge of Severus' household, entered the library and said in his usual nervous fashion that it was getting late, that the litter and the procession were all lined up and waiting, and that the judge should hurry. Severus, switching to Latin, assured

Scorpus he would be right along, and quickly selecting a book for the litter ride to his office, left the library.

On his way to the front hall, Severus stopped into the *tablinum* to say goodbye to his wife, Artemisia. She was a Greek beauty and a Roman citizen. With long dark hair, keen dark eyes, and high cheekbones, she had a face full of intelligence. Her figure was perhaps too slim for the current taste, though not for her husband's. Artemisia had been born and raised in Athens and appropriately had what Homer called "Athena's gifts – talent in handicrafts and a clever mind." The previous month she had been painting portraits; today she was back to working on her biography of Cleopatra. As usual when working, she was dressed in an ordinary gray tunic, clad more like a poor slave than the mistress of the house. "I'm a slave to my studies," she generally countered when challenged about her attire, though she was not entirely joking. The table in front of her was covered with scrolls, tablets, styli, pens and ink, and her lap was occupied by the family cat Phaon, who she was stroking while her thoughts were wandering toward Egypt, 200 years in the past.

Artemisia looked up as Marcus came in. They smiled warmly at each other, exchanged endearments in their private mixture of Latin and Greek, and kissed as warmly as their smiles forecast. Then Severus left for the Forum.

II

A CORPSE IS DISCOVERED

"Go!" commanded the judge's slave way-clearer. He dashed down the street towards the first intersection, shouting "Make way! Make way for the most eminent Marcus Flavius Severus, judge of the Court of the Urban Prefect!" The milling crowd along the narrow street began parting slowly upon hearing the high Equestrian title *"eminentissimus,"* quickened when the word "judge" was barked, and turned into a scramble when "Court of the Urban Prefect" reached their ears. No one was keen on interfering with a procession of a judicial officer; much less was anyone anxious to have an encounter with a judge of a court with criminal jurisdiction. As the crowd parted, the way-clearer stationed himself at the intersection to warn off people and litters approaching from other directions. Four bearers, dressed in red tunics with narrow green *clavi* and green belts, hoisted Severus, settled in his litter, to their shoulders. Two official lictors, supplied by the government, each armed with the *fasces*, a bundle of rods representative of magisterial power, strode in single file leading a parade of tunic-clad slaves and toga-clad citizens who walked fore and aft the litter.

Though Severus enjoyed walking, he loved to ride to work — particularly in his own litter. It was only a four-bearer litter, but it had both modern and traditional features. The traditional ones were its comfort — a fine wool mattress and swan's-down bolster, sumptuous red interior, gold embroidered red canopy and elegant dark wood frame; its modern feature — the translucent sliding windows — enabled the rider to close the sides and yet read inside. The ensemble not only made a grand display, but the easy rhythmic motion of being borne aloft on a comfortable bed made a soothing and luxurious beginning to a day's work.

Severus slid open the window facing two men walking abreast: Glycon, his slave just back from copying the Daily Acts from the news boards in the Old Forum, and Quintus Proculus, his court clerk. The latter gently took Severus' hand and kissed him on the cheek in greeting. The judge wished him well — "*salve*" — and returned the morning kiss. Then, as was his habit, he turned first to Glycon. "What's in the news this morning?"

"*Domine*," said Glycon, visibly excited. "It's all over the City. And I saw it. There was a murder in the forum this morning. I saw the body. It was right there, on the steps of the Temple of Mars the Avenger."

"In the Forum of Augustus?" exclaimed Severus with surprise. "Where my court is?"

"Yes. The *Vigiles* found the body at dawn. It was dumped there during the night. It was all hacked up. The stomach was ripped open, like in the arena, with the insides all over the place. I was going to the Old Forum when I saw a crowd in front of the Temple of Mars. The police doctor was already there, examining the body."

"Who was it?"

"I don't know. No one in the crowd knew. I asked."

"Did you see any of this, Quintus?" asked Severus, addressing his court clerk who had kept pace with the conversation.

"I heard about it, judge," Quintus Proculus acknowledged in a precise manner. He was a thin, wispy man, about sixty years of age. He had spent most of his life in the law courts, recording proceedings in 'Tironian Notes' shorthand, and administering the court files and slaves. Proculus was conscientious to a fault, took pride in maintaining the proprieties and dignity of a Roman court and had an appreciation and love for detail. "I'm afraid," he went on, "that I'm much too squeamish to actually look at such a sight, but I walked by after they took the body away, while the ceremony to purify the temple was going on." He shook his head in bewilderment. "The priests who are in charge of keeping the cult of Mars are furious about the desecration. This is the second sacrilege at the Temple of Mars the Avenger. I remember, judge, when I was a boy, how some criminals once broke into the temple and stole the huge bronze helmet right off the statue of Mars. That's when the Senate voted to transfer the treasure vaults from there to the Temple of Castor because Mars couldn't protect his own property. And now this. It's shocking. The priest took the lance of Mars and clashed it repeatedly against his shield. 'Mars, awake!' he called, over and over again, just like generals at the outbreak of war. They were trying to rouse the god and avenge the crime against his holy place. Perhaps this time it will succeed."

"Perhaps," nodded Severus in a doubting tone. "Still, I think it would be more fruitful to rouse the *vigiles* and the Urban Cohort than a marble statue." He turned to Glycon. "Now tell me what the Daily Acts has to say this morning."

Glycon opened his wax tablet and proceeded to read from his notes, reporting the details of yesterday's house fires, government notices, dispatches from the provinces, and city gossip that appeared on the news boards.

Severus listened with interest while the procession wound its way through the narrower residential and commercial streets, all but lined with high, balconied four, five and six-story red brick apartment houses. The noise of men and women heading for work, children on their way to school, beggars entreating passing litter processions and cries of street hawkers mingled with the hammering from small workshops to create a scene of lively confusion. Smells of hot bread and buns, juicy sausages and warm cakes wafted from cookshops to entice the senses in the morning air, not yet overpowered by the *aer infamis*. Later on in the day this smog would often hover over and stink up the city with noxious vapors from countless burning wood stoves, oil lamps and industrial smelters in use in a city with well over a million inhabitants.

Soon, on a broader avenue which led to the forums, the tenements and small shops became mixed with porticoes, temples, fountains and more elegant stores. The light reflected sharply off the brick and marble which covered most of the concrete buildings, while in the distance, on the hills and in the areas between, loomed the stately aggregation of palaces, baths, basilicas, temples, aqueducts, triumphal arches, statues and forums which formed the center of a vast city and empire.

These hills and places in-between shone a brilliant white, the color broken up by even more brilliant reflections from gilded roof tiles and domes and bronze statuary. The gleam was softened by a sea of red roof tiles, and the whites, golds and reds were smoothed by the restful greenery of trees, gardens and parks throughout the expanse of buildings. Colorful awnings shaded nearly every opening and window, while the whole view was framed by the light blue sky of a clear autumn morning.

By the time Glycon finished with a report of the schedule for the chariot races to take place on the Ides, the judge's procession had slowed to a crawl and joined a line of litters struggling to get through the congestion at the center of the City. Though horses and wheeled vehicles were banned in Rome during the day, the numerous pedestrians and litters were still sufficient to cause the daily traffic jams which often turned a pleasant ride into an aggravating series of delays and waits. Severus, however, was used to it. He closed the sliding window, settled into a comfortable reclining position, opened his book, stared for a moment at the painting of the author on the first page, and began to read.

III

AN AMULET IS FOUND

Judge Severus' court was not in the great hall of a spacious basilica where the most prestigious judges and courts sat, nor was it even located in the modern Forum of Trajan or the hallowed Old Forum where the Senate met. Rather, like many of the courts devoted to public prosecutions, it was housed in the Forum of Augustus in one of the twin colonnades which flanked the Temple of Mars the Avenger.

The white marble temple of Mars was famous for its architectural perfection and the colonnades held the equally famous gallery of the *triumphatores*, more than 100 lifelike statues of everyone who had ever won a triumphal parade through the city of Rome. All the statues were strikingly painted in triumphal dress: face colored red, purple toga emblazoned with gold stars and ivory scepter and laurel wreath in hand. Two famous paintings, old masterworks by the Greek Apelles depicting scenes with Alexander the Great, were also exhibited in the Forum. The only jarring note – a small detail –

was that the face of Alexander had been painted out of the pictures and the face of Augustus substituted. It had been a posthumous tribute by the emperor Claudius to the revered founder of the empire.

It was shortly before the fifth hour when Severus finished his court session, held alongside other courts in public, in the open under the columned portico ringing the forum. He walked briskly to his chambers behind the portico, beginning to unwrap his toga before he was even through the door. Tryphon, his slave-valet who had marched in the morning procession, was waiting to help him unwind the inconvenient garment.

With a smile the judge greeted his two waiting aides, Caius Vulso and Publius Aelianus Straton. Both were members of the Urban Cohort and wore their full dress military uniforms.

Vulso, a centurion, was tall and strong, with craggy almost brutal features, a thick neck, a short, trimmed military beard, and a confident manner. He had spent a full career in the army, having served with eight of the Empire's twenty-eight legions, from the VI Victrix in northern Britain to the XII Fulminata on the Persian frontier. When his twenty-year enlistment was up, he had opted for the 3,000 sesterces cash retirement bonus instead of the land grant, and came to Rome to enlist in the higher paying Urban Cohort. He always carried his centurion's vinewood swagger stick in his hand. It was part of him.

Straton was leaner and shorter, with a fuller beard and a lower rank — *tesserarius*. His name revealed the status of a freedman, once a slave of the imperial house of the last emperor, Publius Aelius Hadrianus. Unlike

Vulso, he was a Greek, and an antagonism often felt among Roman and Hellene lingered between them. Straton, as a slave, had suffered from and was embittered by the dominion of Rome, while Vulso reveled in the power of his people.

Severus sat down on a white-cushioned reading couch. Behind him on the wall was an official portrait of the emperor Antoninus Pius, flanked by the two co-heirs to the throne, Marcus Aurelius and Lucius Verus.

"I've cleared my docket for the rest of the day," he said, sorting some documents and handing them to his clerk, who filed them in the judge's *scrinium*, a tall circular case for records and books which stood in the middle of the office. Then, addressing his aides, he asked if they had made any progress on Fabia's disappearance.

"Have you heard about the murder in the forum this morning?" replied Vulso indirectly.

"Glycon mentioned something about a body that was found on the steps of the Temple of Mars the Avenger."

"I got there before it was taken away," said the centurion, fingering a chain with an amulet attached. "The *Vigiles* have no idea who the corpse is. The man looked to be about forty-years-old. The body was wrapped in a cloak, but naked underneath. He was also a mess. The police doctor estimated he had been stabbed at least thirty times. But since there wasn't all that much blood on the steps, he believes the victim was killed elsewhere and dumped in front of the temple." He lightly tossed the chain amulet on the table in front of the judge's couch. "This was found around the victim's neck."

Severus picked up the amulet and examined it closely. His eyes widened.

"It's a seal stone engraved with a man and a fishing pole and a woman with a crown!" he exclaimed. "Exactly as on the tablet we found in Fabia's bedroom."

"I thought you'd be interested in it." said Vulso smugly.

"Proculus." ordered the judge "give me the message tablet we found in Fabia's bedroom."

The clerk took the tablet from the *scrinium* and handed it to Severus. He opened it and placed the amulet beside the engraving. They matched. Next, fetching a second tablet he pressed the amulet onto the virgin wax, compared the two imprints and passed them around to his aides.

"They're the exact same. The impression on the message-tablet found on Fabia's dressing table was made by this seal. There is no doubt."

"She probably killed the man." snorted Vulso. "In a fit of rage."

"How do you know she wasn't murdered with him?" countered Straton.

"Then where is her body?"

"And where is her slave Phryne?" mused the judge. "No. We must keep our minds open until we have more facts. Anything is possible, so let's not form preconceptions. We will develop theories when we have more to go on. Did you have the police artist make a painting of the victim?"

"It's being done now. Fortunately, all the stab wounds were on the torso. His face was almost unmarked, though twisted into a horrified expression. I suppose they will be able to make a good likeness of what he looked like in happier moments."

"I'll have to inform the Urban Prefect about this," said Severus. He turned to his clerk. "Quintus, send the prefect an urgent message. I must see him this afternoon."

Proculus nodded and made a note on his wax tablet. Turning to his other aide, the judge asked Straton how his investigation went yesterday. "Did you learn anything from Fabia's slaves?"

"I questioned them briefly, judge. There are thirty-two of them. No one knew what the fisherman and queen drawing was. Nor had they seen it before. Frankly, judge, none of them wanted to talk. They know that slaves aren't allowed to testify against their masters, and they were afraid they would get into trouble with either Ferox or Fabia if they did. I tried to explain that they wouldn't be testifying against their masters, only helping in finding their mistress. But they didn't want to run the risk. I'm afraid you will have to question them yourself, perhaps in court."

"Why don't we just haul those slaves in and torture them?" suggested Vulso. "They probably know what it's all about. Slaves always do. Isn't that right, Strato?"

Straton glared at Vulso. "If you're referring again to the misfortune that I was once a slave, I resent it. I am now a free man and a Roman citizen, as good as you, and I prefer the Greek form of my name, if you don't mind."

The judge ignored their quibbling and turned didactic. "Torture is out of the question, Vulso. I'm obligated by Imperial Rescripts not to begin an investigation with harsh measures. I can't use it until a slave is a suspect and the evidence is so strong that just a confession is lacking. And just recently the emperor issued a new rescript confirming that no torture of slaves be used, except if the truth cannot be reached in any other way. So not only would I be violating the law, but I would also be responsible under the Lex Aquilia to Ferox for any loss in money value of the slaves if they're injured because of torture I ordered. I know these are prosperous times, but I'm not that wealthy. However I will question them." He turned to his clerk. "Quintus, issue court orders for the appearance of Fabia's slaves in my courtroom tomorrow morning. Perhaps one of them might recognize a painting of the murder victim. Vulso, do you have the pictures of Fabia and Phryne yet?"

Vulso unrolled two paintings. "I had the police artist accompany me to the Ferox home. There was a marble bust of Fabia from which he copied her image. The one of Phryne was made from descriptions of the other slaves. I'm having the pictures copied and shown around in the haunts of the Subura district to the usual informers, and to shopkeepers, apartment house porters and neighborhood ward leaders."

Severus examined the paintings carefully. Phryne was blonde, with blue-green eyes; Fabia brunette, with large brown eyes. Both were beautiful women; Phryne in a soft and sensual way, Fabia more blatant and challenging.

"As you can see," commented the centurion, "the slave is unusually striking."

Severus nodded in agreement. He studied the picture of Fabia again. "This one looks dissolute, don't you think so?"

Vulso shrugged. "I officially alerted the *Vigiles* and the Urban Cohorts. They'll be on special lookout for

Fabia and Phryne." He dropped his voice slightly. "I also asked the Imperial Secret Service if they know anything. It's unlikely, but we may learn something useful. You never know who the *curiosi* suspect, whose letters they read or what information they have."

The judge turned to Straton. "Did you canvass the neighborhood of the Ferox mansion?"

"I did, judge. In particular, I spoke to the neighborhood children at play in front of the house. One, a little boy with a scooter, said he saw the lady of the house and a woman slave leave just after the lunch siesta. They went in the direction of the Vicus Tuscus silk market. I tried to trace them by asking shopkeepers and street idlers along the route, but turned up nothing."

"All right," interjected Severus. "Straton, I want you to get a list of Fabia's friends and discreetly start asking questions. She may have confided something to someone. Vulso, you follow up on the murder in the forum this morning. You can tell the *Vigiles* that I'm in charge of the investigation. Don't arch your eyebrows. I know I'm not assigned to it yet, but after I meet with the Urban Prefect this afternoon, I will be."

IV

SEVERUS VISITS THE BATHS AND TALKS TO THE PREFECT

The clear, sunny morning had changed to a gray, drizzling afternoon. Severus' litter was borne up a slope of the Esquiline Hill amidst the crowds streaming to the main southern entrance of the Baths of Trajan. The judge stepped out and paused in the rain to admire the view, centering on the vast, oval Flavian Amphitheater below. Though the scene of gladiatorial combats was being refurbished, and its exterior of marble and statuary was masked by scaffolding, the panorama of the City from the top of the hill was breathtaking.

Preceded by his lictors and followed by slaves, the judge swept through the parting mob lined up at the narrow entrance gate, waiting to pay their small admission coin to the gate attendant.

"Tryphon," Severus said to his slave-valet once they were inside the building, "let the bearers off to enjoy the Baths, while you look around and see if the prefect has arrived yet. You'll find me around here."

Tryphon hurried through the huge main hall, while Severus paused to take in the magnificent interior view and the bustle and activity of the bath-goers.

Though it was only one among the sixteen huge government owned public baths – *thermae* –, and some 900 government licensed private ones in the City of Rome, the Baths of Trajan were the most spectacular. It was in essence a luxurious resort in the middle of the City. And it was for everyone, slaves included. Compliments of the government.

One of the greatest creations of the famous architect Apollodorus of Damascus, the Baths were a huge complex including a sports paleastra with fields for throwing discus and javelin, for ball games, for running and wrestling and for exercising with weights. Slender porticoes ringed the open spaces on three sides enclosing large monumental fountains, along with gardens with pathways for walking and benches for sitting. There were also Greek and Latin libraries in the porticoes, providing scope for pursuing the Roman ideal of a sound mind in a sound body.

The main building was a huge concourse with a high domed ceiling with openings for sunlight to pour in, softly illuminating the whole spacious interior. Bright frescoes enlivened the upper walls with color, while the beautifully marbled, mosaic floor was planted with trees and shrubbery. Rome's "second population", the lifelike painted statuary which rivalled the city's human population in number, was everywhere. Slaves and bath attendants with trays of hot and cold food and drinks passed busily through the main hall calling out their wares to the chattering crowd which, at this hour of the day, was restricted to men only. In one area of the concourse youths frolicked in wrestling and boxing or exercised with weights. In another, ball games were in progress. Groups of bath-goers discussed and argued about the gladiatorial games or chariot races, or current events or transacted business or gossiped, while others listened, admiringly or jeeringly, to declaiming real and would-be philosophers or rhetoricians. Tourists gaped at the decorated ceiling and followed guided tours of the monumental baths. Others, like Severus, were content to stroll about taking in the noisy and tumultuous scene, stopping here and there to watch musicians or dancers, acrobats or jugglers, all performing for the coins the onlookers cared to give them. The Baths were a modern technological marvel for the refreshment, relaxation and enjoyment of the whole populace.

Severus hailed a merchant and bought a slice of toasted honey bread and a Lucanian sausage. He glanced at a famous group sculpted more than 200 years before by the Rhodian artist Agesander and his sons, Polydorus and Athenodorus, depicting Lacoon, the Trojan priest of Apollo, and his two children being crushed to death by snakes.

Severus took a bite of his snack and idly watched three men playing 'intercept' with a large green ball. He was still watching when Tryphon wound his way back from the baths area and reported that the prefect was in the *frigidarium* – the large unheated central hall with its large unheated swimming pool.

On this cold, wet Autumn afternoon, Severus would have preferred the prefect were in the *tepidarium* warm room or the *caldarium* hot tub or even the *sudatorium* steam room, although Severus basically disliked the steam room as too suffocating. Nevertheless, he followed Tryphon into the dressing room, found an empty cubbyhole, handed his clothes to his slave and, shivering in anticipation, strode naked into the *frigidarium*.

Making his way into the huge, noisy, crowded hall, he saw the prefect just coming out of the swimming pool. Like everyone else, he too was nude. The baths were one place of 'equality', at least in theory, in a class conscious society, where everyone was without the clothes that usually bore signs of wealth or poverty, citizenship or foreignness, high or low status. Emperors born into the highest social class and slaves born into slavery all appeared naked in the baths and therefore in some sense appeared to be equal, except of course for those either under-endowed or over-endowed whose appearances often brought reactions from the crowd ranging from laughter to applause.

As he walked toward the prefect, who was now seated on a bench and being dried off by his slaves with towels and blankets, Severus ignored the furtive glances his trim figure and shapely legs attracted from those bathgoers for whom bathing was secondary. Not that that wasn't always the case, but it was only the last emperor Hadrian who changed the policy on mixed gender nude bathing that had been the rule for many years. Nowadays, it was women in the morning and men in the afternoon. Severus preferred the old system.

The prefect politely rose when he saw Severus approach.

"*Salve*, Quintus Lollius Urbicus," said Severus as he took the prefect's hand and kissed him on the cheek.

"*Salve*, Marcus Flavius Severus," said Urbicus, returning the kiss.

The prefect was a husky, robust man with a florid face and the harassed mien and often distanced look of an overworked official addicted to *theriac* – the popular opium based 'tranquility' and 'cure-all' pills. "Sit down," invited Urbicus, "and look at these two buffoons on their knees with their hands tied behind their backs, trying to bend over backwards and touch the floor. Even at my age I can still do it."

"Undoubtedly your long years in the army," suggested Severus. The prefect sat down and motioned Severus to join him. He did, clenching his teeth as his bare behind hit the cold marble bench.

"Severus," said the prefect, as one of his slaves poured a vial of perfume over Severus' head, "have you heard about the murder last night in the Forum of Augustus? All Rome is talking about it."

"Of course, prefect. In fact, that's what I wanted to talk to you about."

"A desecration!" exclaimed the prefect, his voice rising in anger and his face growing red. "And what's even more of a desecration is the incompetence in the VIth precinct of *Vigiles* which is supposed to be patrolling the Forums area. I had the prefect of the *Vigiles* in my office most of the morning and made him explain it to me, since I'll have to explain it to the emperor. I ordered him to transfer the whole patrol on duty last night to the XIV Region across the Tiber. By Hercules! If they can't guard an empty forum at night, let's see how they like patrolling the streets of the oriental and Jewish sections of the City in the dark."

He took a bean-size lump of 'tranquility' from a box one of his slaves extended to him, swallowed it, composed himself, and extended an arm toward the judge. "But you said you wanted to talk to me about that murder."

"Prefect, perhaps we had better continue our conversation in one of the reading rooms, since I now have information that the murder in the forum is connected to the case you assigned me to investigate yesterday. And I also have some exhibits to show you that will prove it."

Urbicus gave him a surprised look.

"Clear out one of those reading rooms," he addressed a slave. "I want to talk to Judge Severus alone."

Severus breathed a small sigh of relief that he would be heading to someplace warmer. They parted to change into their tunics and meet in a few minutes. The judge hurried to the dressing room and told Tryphon to get him a cup of calda. The hot wine and water drink, charged with spices, would do him good. His teeth were chattering with cold.

"What happened?" asked the prefect when they were comfortably settled on adjoining reading room couches. Urbicus' brow was furrowed with concern.

Severus produced the message tablet found in Fabia's bedroom, the amulet from the murder victim's neck, and the tablet with the fresh seal impression from the amulet, filling in the prefect as he displayed the evidence. "Identical," he summed up. "The message she received was made by the victim's seal."

The prefect studied the objects, looking back and forth from the tablets to the amulet.

"And now he's dead and she's disappeared," he sighed, his shoulders drooping. "What is to be done about it?"

"Find out as much as we can. For a start, I'd like to know what you know about the senator's wife."

"Not much. It's the senator who I know."

"Then please tell me about him."

The prefect eased onto his elbow. He talked in a relaxed manner as the opium in the 'tranquility' pill took effect.

"It's about twenty-five years now since I first met Ferox. We both served with Hadrian on the expedition to crush the revolt in Judaea, or Palaestina as we're officially supposed to call it nowadays. We were with the Legion X Fretensis." His eyes took on a far away look. "What a campaign that was!" he said, as if half enjoying and half dreading the memory. "Ferox and I became friends. Army buddies. We got into scrapes together, fights, women, you know what I mean. As a young man — as a soldier — Ferox was brave and daring, perhaps even to the point of foolhardiness. He was also hot-tempered and willful, and he displayed a certain arrogance about his ancestry and powerful connections. Everybody, even his military superiors, were a little afraid of him. Shortly after we returned from the war Ferox married Fabia. She was a beautiful young child, about fifteen-years-old. Ferox was in his thirties and had escaped marriage until then through his obstinacy. But he had squandered his inheritance through escapades and high living, and marriage to a large dowry seemed the way out. It was intended to be a marriage of convenience. But the gods, Marcus, confound us all. Despite the age difference, or perhaps because of it. Ferox conceived a violent passion for Fabia. I remember it well. My friends and I used to chide him for his obsession with such a young and inexperienced girl. He would fly into a rage whenever we joked about it. He was entranced by her."

"It was about that time I began to take up various government posts that kept me from Rome, so I lost touch with Ferox. But about six years later, as I chanced to be passing through Ephesus, I learned that Ferox was serving there on some imperial commission. He had brought his wife along. I stayed in their house for a few days. Even then I noticed his fascination for her. His eyes wouldn't leave her whenever they were in the same room."

"Did she return his ardor?"

"I was never able to tell, though I often wondered about it. Last night I discussed it with my wife, and she remembered her impression at the time was that Fabia felt flattered by all the attention. But my wife thought it would not last, that Ferox was too domineering, too suffocating, too possessive. In recent years, Ferox has been ill and withdrawn. As for Fabia, she has matured into a woman of her own. The last time my wife and I saw them was at a dinner party at their house about a year ago. Let me tell you about it, Marcus. You may find it interesting."

The prefect sat up on his couch, while Severus reclined on his elbow.

"Ferox almost died that year. He had been very sick. The doctors had given up hope, although, of course, that doesn't mean too much. They bled him, tried a thousand different herbs and drugs, everything they could think

of. They also prescribed music as a remedy, first flutes
and then the seven-stringed lyre, the harmony of the four
tones. And that seemed to work. At least he somehow
recovered, and from that day on he declared himself a
new man. He said he had given up his old habits and
beliefs. He leads the life of an old Republican – stingy,
virtuous, straight as an arrow, thinks he's Cato the Elder
– you know the type. He says he lives according to the
Stoic precept of *gravitas*. He lost his temper and became
strangely unemotional, cold and icy."

"In what way?"

"There was an incident at this dinner party. It was
held to celebrate Ferox' recovery and his devotion to
philosophy. It was a customary banquet, nine guests, a
few of them philosophers, or at least guests who dressed
in old rags and made sounds like philosophers. I think
Ferox was trying to show off his new life style – you
know, a large pot of Egyptian beans with small pieces
of cucumbers and squash for food, spiced with preten-
tious conversation about linguistics and philology – the
definitions and derivations of words used by Cato or
Seneca or some Greek Stoic or other – a conversation
that always bores me. Whenever I tried to bring up the
good old days in the army or the chariot races, he would
look at me as if I were a dullard." He hesitated. "What
are you laughing about, Severus?" Did I say something
funny?"

"Not intentionally, Prefect," replied Severus. "But
after I finished studying law here in Rome, I spent a year
attending the lectures of the rhetorician Calvisius Taurus
in Athens. He would sometimes invite his students to
dinner and serve the same food and talk. I always felt the

austerity of those dinners was as ostentatious as if he had served flamingo. Well, if we are fed ostentation, let it at least be with flamingo instead of beans."

"You've struck it with the needle," said Urbicus colloquially, "that's exactly what I thought at the time."

"But I interrupted you," apologized Severus. "You were talking about Ferox' coldness."

"Ah, yes. As I was saying, Severus, I had dinner at his house. Fabia was there too, as I remember. Anyway, during the dinner a slave committed some offense or other and Ferox gave orders that he be whipped right in front of the guests. This slave was apparently versed in philosophy himself, and when they began to whip him, he protested that he had done nothing wrong and didn't deserve to be beaten. As the whipping continued, he changed his tune and began to yell, not shrieks and groans, but rebukes. He called Ferox a disgrace to philosophy. He yelled that Ferox had often called anger shameful and to whip someone in a fit of anger contradicted his professed beliefs. He finally called Ferox a hypocrite, over and over again."

"I hardly blame him," commented Severus softly.

"Well, Ferox just smiled and in a cold unemotional way asked the slave what made him think he was angry. 'Is it my expression, my voice, my color, or even my words that make you think I am consumed by anger? My opinion is that my eyes are not wild, my expression is not disturbed, I am neither shouting madly nor foaming at the mouth nor getting red in the face. I am not trembling from anger or making violent gestures.' I remember his words quite well because Ferox then turned to the slave who had stopped the whipping and ordered him to resume. 'You,' he said, 'keep at it while this thing and I are debating.'

"I thought the whole exhibition was in bad taste,quite out of tune with our modern notions of *humanitas*, with the 'spirit of our time' as Trajan used to call it.   But Ferox' philosopher friends seemed to appreciate it.   Not so Fabia.   She turned pale.   My wife said that her face was like chalk, that her eyes blazed at him with hatred. Afterwards, after the slave was beaten into unconsciousness, Ferox and his friends cheerfully entered into a discussion on the subtle differences in meaning between the Latin and Greek words for 'anger'."

"That's certainly not the Stoicism I learned," remarked Severus.   He was both startled and disturbed by the story.   "From what you say, Prefect, the senator seems perfectly capable of killing his wife and dumping her lover on the steps of a temple devoted to vengeance. He may be icy instead of hot-tempered now, but in either case he seems unbalanced."

"I realize he may be capable of it," rejoined the prefect, "but we have no proof that he did anything, or that she's dead, or even that this murdered man was her lover.   There may be some other reason for what happened.   And besides, Severus, I don't see how he could have done it.   He was away at his country villa for the past week and it's almost half a day's ride from the City. So how could he know his wife disappeared or where she went, let alone have murdered her?"

"I'll report to you after I speak to him," remarked Severus.

"Yes, I suppose you'll have to question him.   I ordered Fabia's slave – when he reported her disappearance to me – to refrain from telling Ferox what had happened. I took the chance she would return, in which case it would be better for her not to have her husband know about her absence. But now she's still missing, and there's been a murder..."

A slave holding a small sun dial in the palm of his hand opened the door to the reading room and looked at the prefect with an expression that said it was time to go. Urbicus rose from his couch, extended a hand to Severus to walk with him and headed toward the door. "I'm sorry to rush off," he explained, "but I'm squeezing you in between meetings with the Prefect of Vehicles and the Prefect of Child Welfare." They stopped outside the door of the reading room, surrounded by the bustle and clamor of the main concourse. "Keep me closely informed about developments, Severus. Despite what I've told you, Ferox is still an old friend and I feel a loyalty."

"I will. And, Prefect, should I assume that I am officially assigned by you to investigate the murder in the forum as well?"

"You don't have to assume it. I give you the *cognitio*. It's your case as of right now."

With that, the prefect downed another dose of 'tranquility' and dashed off in a cloud of attendants for his next meeting.

V

ALEXANDER EXPLAINS
THE FISHERMAN AND QUEEN

"What interests me most about the prefect's story," said Alexander that night, "is that Fabia lived in Ephesus."

Severus, Artemisia and Alexander reclined comfortably on each of three purple cushioned couches in the *triclinium* dining room. Severus wore a casual red tunic with white *clavi*; he had removed his belt about two-thirds of the way through dinner. Artemisia was dressed elegantly in a v-necked white Greek dress, with white shoes embroidered in gold, an ivory and gold arm bracelet from India, and a blue faiance Egyptian necklace. Her dark hair fell loosely below her shoulders. Alexander wore a yellow-orange tunic with black *clavi* and a black belt.

The house slaves had cleared away dinner, leaving wine and fruit on the table between the couches. Numerous oil lamps hanging from tall bronze stands glowed softly, illuminating the wall frescoes where birds merrily perched among trees and flowers in soft shades of blue, green and yellow. Occasionally the steady glow was brushed aside by a waft of air or some gentle movement of the lamps, causing the flames to flicker, dim and then flare, throwing fantastic shadows onto the walls.

"Oh?" said Severus, surprised at Alexander's remark. "Why is it important that she lived in Ephesus?"

"He discovered something," suggested Artemisia. "I saw him come home this afternoon with a pile of scrolls. And since then he's been walking around the house with a smug smile, looking, as the saying goes, like he has Jupiter by the balls."

"It's true," laughed Alexander. "I went to three libraries today, did research, discussed the problem with librarians, and then I found the answer to the fisherman and queen riddle."

"Wonderful!" exclaimed Severus. "Tell me about it. It has to do with Ephesus, I assume?"

Alexander nodded. "I know neither of you has been in Ephesus, but you've heard it is a fine city, the largest in the province of Asia."

"I know it has street lighting at night," said Artemisia.

"Yes. And there are beautiful works of art, paintings and statuary all over the place. One painting in particular is of note, renowned even, and it's still exhibited in the harbor."

"And it has to do with a fisherman and a queen?" prompted Artemisia.

"Let me tell you the story. It may explain a few things." He took a sip of wine. "Almost 500 years ago, after Alexander the Great had conquered the East, his successor Seleucus ruled in Syria, Persia and Asia Minor, as you well know. It seems that a rash young painter, named Ctesicles, became angry because the queen, Stratonike, did not give him a sufficiently honorable reception at court. So, to retaliate and win himself notoriety, if not fame, he secretly painted a picture of the queen romping with a certain fisherman who, gossip had it, was her lover. Then, just before he jumped on a ship leaving Ephesus, Ctesicles placed the painting on public exhibition at the Ephesus harbor. When the queen first heard about it, she was furious. But to everyone's surprise and delight, when she actually saw the painting she would not allow it to be removed, saying that the likeness of the two figures was 'admirably expressed.' The picture is still there and everyone in Ephesus knows the story."

"So that's the origin of the fisherman and queen symbols," mused Severus.

"It must be," said Alexander confidently. "The more so since the prefect told you that Fabia lived in Ephesus."

"Fabia and the murdered man must have been lovers," commented Artemisia, "just like Stratonike and her fisherman. And after what the prefect revealed about her husband, I'm not surprised."

"In these days," said Severus wryly, "she hardly needs the excuse."

The comment provoked Artemisia. "Fabia has a right to live her own life if she chooses. These are modern times. Even Roman Stoics like Musonius Rufus, not to mention Plato, think women should be educated the same as men. They have the same souls. So, women shouldn't be kept in seclusion anymore and Fabia can take a lover."

Severus backed off. "I didn't say women aren't supposed to lead their own lives. I was only thinking about the morals of the times, or lack of them. You can't tell me that license in our society hasn't led to the breakdown of the family. Look at the divorce rate."

"I hope you're not going to quote Seneca or Juvenal about women." She mimicked Seneca's professorial voice and oratorical gestures. "'Illustrious ladies reckon the year not by the names of the consuls but by those of their husbands. They divorce in order to re-marry. They marry in order to divorce.' What nonsense! Just let a woman try a case in court or race in Greek Games or even discuss military or legal affairs and men begin trotting out those so-called social critics to bewail the breakdown of society. In my opinion, most of the problems are caused by men who cling to outmoded ways than by women who seek interesting lives outside the home. And in any event, the morality of today is not nearly as bad as it was 100 years ago. Just compare Antoninus Pius, the emperor now, with Nero, the emperor then."

"That may be true, but there are many men who feel threatened by women rivalling them intellectually and others are put off by a woman who takes up fencing and wrestling, though, as you know, I'm not one of them."

"I wouldn't have married you otherwise."

"But you must admit that in the rush to emulate men, many women acquire men's vices instead of their strengths."

"It wouldn't be any fun if we couldn't have the vices too," she laughed. "But as for Fabia, you don't know whether she took a lover because she acquired one of her husband's vices or simply to escape from them."

"That's so. But the question is not whether Fabia was right or wrong in taking a lover. She obviously had her reasons. The question is why her 'fisherman' has turned up in Rome, years later, as a corpse."

He rose from his couch and extended an arm to Artemisia. She playfully let herself be pulled up. "Tomorrow," he added. "Fabia's slaves will be in court. I'm sure some of them were with the illustrious senator and his child bride in Ephesus."

Artemisia laughed and snuggled up to her husband. He embraced her and they exchanged lustful smiles and began running their hands all over each other on the way out.

"Please let me know what happens tomorrow," called Alexander to their backs. "You can take it from me, slaves always know something."

They would have agreed, had they been listening.

FOUR DAYS BEFORE THE IDES

VI

JUDGE SEVERUS HOLDS COURT

Judge Severus had his courtroom set up for a private inquiry in a room behind the portico in the Forum of Augustus.

At the third hour court was called into session and Judge Severus took his customary place on the magistrate's chair, a folding stool without arms or back. The chair was set on the 'tribunal', a platform which raised the judge slightly above the level of everyone else. The tribunal area was located in a semi-circular apse which faced benches immediately in front where parties, witnesses, lawyers and, behind them, spectators could sit.

Seated on stools arranged to the side and behind the judge were his aides, Vulso and Straton, and the court clerk Proculus, who was taking down the proceedings in 'Tironian Notes'. At one side of the apse was a statue of Jupiter Fidius, the god of Good Faith, whose image graced all Roman courts. On the other side was a large water clock used for measuring the time allotted to lawyers for their speeches. Severus' two official lictors stood at attention at either side of the tribunal.

The judge ordered the courtroom cleared of spectators who had heard gossip about a backroom hearing and had pushed into the room before anything started. Grumbling court buffs and idlers who regularly made the rounds of the criminal courts looking for scandal and excitement and a news reporter who covered the criminal courts for the Daily Acts were summarily turned out.

Severus addressed Proculus.

"This is for the record. I am now beginning the *cognitio* – the official inquiry – into the murder of an unknown person who was found yesterday on the steps of the Temple of Mars the Avenger. Call as the first witness, the slave Menelaus."

An old man was led by two court officers to stand before the tribunal. His hair was sparse and white and he appeared physically and mentally weak and worn out. Wrinkled skin, tired eyes deep set into their sockets and a frail frame made him look almost sorrowful. Only his expensive silk tunic showed that things weren't always that bad.

"Name and status," rang out the clerk, his voice echoing off the marble floor.

"Menelaus, chief slave in the *familia* of Senator Lucius Junius Ferox." A slight despondency sounded in his tone.

"How did you come to your present position?" asked Judge Severus from the tribunal.

"I was born a slave, *eminentissime,* in the house of Fabia's father. He is a banker in Cremona and a member of the Equestrian order. I was given to Fabia as a wedding present. I have been fortunate in finding favor in the eyes of my mistress and master over the years and I was promoted to chief slave two years ago."

"If I have any hope of finding your mistress, Menelaus, I'll need your help and the help of all the other slaves. In particular, I'll have to know private things about her, things you wouldn't normally talk about." Severus' tone was mild and patient. "I'm sure you're aware of the legal principle that slaves may not testify against their masters. But I can assure you that you have nothing to fear on that account. The law allows you to testify on behalf of your mistress, in aid of her. What you tell me today would not be testifying against Fabia, but for her. Do you understand?"

"I do, *eminentissime*."

"Good. Then I would appreciate it, Menelaus, if you would also instruct the other slaves in the importance of candor. Only by knowing the truth about Fabia will we be able to find her. You must understand that to reveal confidences is now in your mistress' interest. She would want you to do so. No one will be punished. I will see to it."

"I realize it is in her interest, *eminentissime*. I will do my best and I will tell the others to do the same."

"Thank you, Menelaus," said the judge brightly. "Now tell me about her. You say she is the daughter of a banker in Cremona. Tell me what she was like as a child."

"As a child?" He was taken aback by the question. "As a child she was like any other little girl. She was prettier than most, though, and somewhat moody. She would be overly happy one moment and overly sad

another. But she was given a good education – she was
sent to school and then had private tutors. Her father
wanted to make her eligible for a good marriage, one that
would improve the family's social status. He put away a
large dowry for that purpose."

"Tell me about her marriage to Senator Ferox."

"When Fabia was fifteen, her father wrote to friends
in Rome to find a suitable husband. Senator Ferox was
recommended. He was thirty-five at the time and had
just returned from the war in Judaea. Fabia readily gave
her legal consent and they were married in Rome the
same year."

"What has Fabia done in the twenty years since the
marriage? Are there any children?"

"No, *eminentissime*. There was one that died in
childbirth about a year after the marriage and there were
two miscarriages in the next two years."

"Has the family lived in Rome all these years?"

"Yes, in the Caelian Hill house, except for three
years when the senator was with an Imperial Commission in the East."

"Tell me about that, Menelaus. Where did he go?"

"To Ephesus, *eminentissime*. I believe the commission was sent out to redress grievances of mismanagement
brought by the citizens of the province of Asia. The commission toured various cities in the province, inspected
finances, organized public works and political and financial
affairs. It was based in Ephesus and the family was given
a house in the city. I went along as one of Fabia's slaves."

"Did Fabia like it there?"

"Oh yes, *eminentissime*. She was very happy there.
We arrived the year after the second miscarriage and her

mood changed noticeably. The early years in Rome – the pregnancy problems – had been hard on her. In Ephesus she had more freedom, the senator being frequently away with the commission, and she went out all the time to enjoy the wares and attractions of the city. She became a devotee of the theater and of the cult of Isis. She is still an avid follower of both."

"Did you return to Rome after Ephesus?"

"Yes, *eminentisssime*. That was seventeen years ago. Ferox took up a seat in the Senate and Fabia resumed life in the Caelian Hill house. But two years ago the senator fell seriously ill and barely recovered. He has been in retirement since then and now lives a secluded life, either in Rome or at his villa outside the city."

"Does Fabia spend most of her time at home? What is her daily routine like, Menelaus?"

"She sleeps late in the morning and spends much of her time in the bazaars or at the theater or in devotion to the Isis cult. But then there are days when she never comes out of her room, sometimes many of them in a row."

"What has her mood been recently, in the week before her disappearance, for instance?"

"She was nervous. On edge. It was a little unusual, especially because she had been in a very good mood the week before. I remember she had gone to the bazaar every day. One day to the silk market, another to the Via Lata jewelry shops. She was on a buying spree. New clothes, jewelry, perfumes. But in the days before she disappeared she was very tense. She hardly ate a thing. She stayed in her room and wanted to know who it was

every time someone came to the door. Then the message-tablet arrived for her and she left in a hurry."

"Menelaus" said the judge leaning forward, "I want
to remind you of our little agreement before I ask the
next question. It is imperative that you answer it as hon-
estly as possible, no matter how private it may be."

"I remember, *eminentissime*. I will answer."

"It is not entirely unknown, Menelaus," the judge
began carefully, "that fashionable ladies, like your mistress, have, shall we say, flirtations with men other than
their husbands. Has this perhaps also been the case with
Fabia?"

Menelaus looked at the floor.

"I need your cooperation," prodded Severus.

"How can I tell you, *eminentissime*. I took an oath
to Apollo."

"I will arrange to have priests intercede."

Menelaus' face was twisted with indecision.

"It's very important," urged Severus.

The slave's face relaxed. "Yes. She has had flirtations."

"The names, Menelaus," ordered the judge.

"I only know five, *eminentissime*. There may have
been others." He ran his hand through his hair. "The
first was in Ephesus. His name was Anaximander. He
was a young man, no older than Fabia. He was a poor
artisan, a mosaicist, if I remember correctly, with hopes
of becoming an actor. He had been hired to repair a broken floor in the house we had. That's how they met. I
noticed the change in Fabia right away. She fell in love,
as the saying goes, like a cockroach into a basin. The

affair lasted for the three years we stayed in the East. But, of course, it ended when we returned to Rome."

"Menelaus, did the senator know about this affair?"

"I am not sure. All I know is that Fabia rarely carried on the affair at the house, even when Ferox and the commission were away from Ephesus. She usually stayed at Anaximander's. It was a small apartment, I remember, near the Temple of Serapis. After we returned from Ephesus there were no other men that I know of, at least for a while. She had been happy with Anaximander and I don't think she could forget him easily. But time wears away memory, and in the past few years there have been others." Menelaus looked from the floor to the judge. "She had a long affair with a man named Publius Planta. He was of the Senatorial class, *eminentissime*. A social friend of the family. It lasted until about two years ago, shortly before Senator Ferox had his illness. Poor Planta had a terrible accident. He fell from the balcony of his apartment one night and was killed. Fabia was distraught for a long time."

"Have there been others since the death of Planta?"

"There have been three others that I am aware of. One was a soldier more than a year ago. He was the son of a friend of the senator. The soldier was visiting Rome on assignment from his legion and stayed at our house. It lasted for a month and then he had to return to the frontier."

"What was his name and legion?"

"His name is Sextus Anicius Metellus and he was stationed at Bonn on the Rhine frontier. I don't know the legion."

Severus turned to Vulso, who informed him that Bonn was the headquarters of the Legion I Minervia.

"She also had an affair with a Greek philosopher who often stays at the house as a guest of Ferox. His name is Timotheus. He travels about a lot but I think he has a hovel in the Subura."

"And the third one?"

"I am ashamed to say it, *eminentissime*. But Fabia had an affair with one of the household slaves. His name is Croesus."

Severus turned to his clerk who handed him a tablet containing the list of the slaves in Ferox' household.

"I don't see his name on this list," said the judge. "Where is Croesus now?"

"He was sold, your honor, to the slave dealer Squilla, in the slave market behind the Temple of Castor. He had broken an expensive glass bowl, of the kind the Greeks call blood-red ware. Ferox had him whipped for it, *eminentissime*, and then sold him."

Severus again turned to his clerk. "Let me have the painting," he said.

Proculus unfurled a papyrus roll and presented it to the judge. Severus looked thoughtfully at the face of the man found murdered on the steps of the Temple of Mars the Avenger. He handed it to a court officer.

"Show him the painting... Menelaus, please look carefully at the portrait and tell me if you know the man."

Severus and his aides saw the look of confusion on Menelaus' face change to amazement and recognition.

"It's Anaximander," he said simply.

VII

A LETTER TO THE PREFECT

Marcus Flavius Severus, Judge, sends many a greeting to Quintus Lollius Urbicus, Prefect of the City:

I have learned the identity of the body found on the steps of the Temple of Mars the Avenger. His name was Anaximander. You will see from the transcript of the slave Menelaus' testimony that Anaximander and Fabia were lovers in Ephesus when she lived there. I have also traced the fisherman and queen symbols to a piece of local Ephesian lore and it confirms that relationship.

I spent all day today questioning thirty slaves belonging to Senator Ferox and Fabia. What I learned was both highly informative and deeply disturbing.

Perhaps the lack of harmony in the Caelian Hill house was most visibly conveyed by the dress of the slaves. Ferox' slaves look like they had undergone a forcible Stoic conversion to extreme frugality. Their clothes were coarse and rough, almost threadbare. Fabia's slaves, on the other hand, flaunted a taste in silks. They were dressed fashionably and extravagantly. The parade of shabbily dressed slaves alternating with slaves wearing the most expensive and stylish tunics was remarked upon by everyone in the courtroom today.

Prefect, I am sorry to say that Senator Ferox is a harsh master. He has taken the discipline of slaves recommended by Cato the Elder to an ugly extreme. I have encountered several cases of flogging besides the one you witnessed at the dinner party and all were ordered for trivial infringements of a harsh regimen. Ferox insists that the slaves be allowed out of the house only for errands. They have to report punctually to Menelaus when they leave and return and their movements are even recorded in a ledger for the senator's inspection.

Moreover the workload of each of his slaves is onerous. While formerly there were 150 slaves in his entourage, the senator's "Stoicism" has led him to sell them off, a few at a time. He now has twelve of his own left and he demands they do the work of three or four slaves apiece. One slave, Probus by name, was formerly the senator's reader. This slave is now required not only to read books to Ferox, but to serve as the senator's secretary, librarian, copyist and keeper of the household animals which, I am informed, includes two dogs, one magpie, a small monkey and three snakes. Probus is also compelled to enforce silence in the house at all times. The slaves are not permitted to speak to each other, except when required by household affairs. It is vintage Cato, I know, but out of place and even disgraceful to be seen in these days.

In the basement of the mansion, Prefect, there is an *ergastulum* for the punishment of slaves. It is a small windowless room which Ferox insists never be cleaned.

Into it he throws recalcitrant slaves for days at a time as a punishment, where they languish among bugs and rats and the soilage of former inmates. I need say no more.

Fabia's slaves, on the other hand, are free to converse and she is lax in her personal demands upon them. She has never ordered a flogging or used the senator's basement cell. The ordinary slap or scolding is her manner of discipline. From the slave's viewpoint, the Caelian Hill house is really two houses – Ferox' and Fabia's. This division, I gather, is but an echo of the relationship between the senator and his wife. It is a tense and bitter one.

I closely questioned one slave about the senator's illness two years ago when, as you know, he almost died. I wasn't so much interested in the nature of the sickness as in Fabia's attentiveness or lack of it during that time. For the illness of one spouse often evokes true feelings from the other.

The slave I questioned, Harpax by name, reported an unusual incident. It was after a particularly bad day. The doctors had been there for hours and talked to Fabia that night with wringing hands and grave expressions. They believed Ferox was near death.

After the doctors left, Fabia told Harpax to go out and bring back a sprig of cypress. Harpax said he scoured the neighborhood until he found a cypress tree in a nearby park. When he returned to the house, Fabia brought him into Ferox' sickroom and told him to hang the cypress above the doorway. While the slave was on the ladder hanging the branch, he saw Fabia waken her husband and tell him there was no hope. She pointed to the symbol of death that Harpax was fixing to the door and then

left the room. The senator understood because his eyes
went wild. Like a cornered animal, the slave put it.

Other slaves testified that after Ferox had recovered,
Fabia stayed in her room for more than a week, barely
touching food.

Since then the senator and his wife talk to each other
only to argue or threaten or humiliate. There have been
several incidents reported by the slaves, one of which
had to do with the flogging you witnessed at the dinner party last year. I questioned the slaves about it and
learned the full story.

The slave who you saw whipped was called Croesus.
You will notice, Prefect, that the transcript of Menelaus'
testimony names this Croesus as one of Fabia's lovers.
Unfortunately for him, he was also the property of her
husband.

While preparing for the dinner party you attended,
Croesus accidentally broke a glass bowl of blood-red
ware. Ferox said nothing about it at the time, but a few
hours later, during the banquet, he had the slave publicly
punished. After you and the other guests left, the senator had Croesus hauled back into the dining room and
in front of Fabia declared his intention to sell him to a
farm chain gang. He told her, one the slaves said, that
if it weren't for Hadrian's Law he would have sold him
to a gladiator's school to be chopped up in the arena or
else killed him himself. Fabia, the slave told me, became
hysterical and began to beat on Ferox with her fists.
Ferox just laughed at her, but when she landed a blow
that stung him, he kicked her in the stomach and left her
lying crumpled on the floor. The next morning Ferox

had Croesus delivered to a slave dealer with instructions to be sold to a chain gang.

I will recount one more incident, Prefect, bearing on our case. It concerns the slave girl Phryne, the one who has disappeared along with Fabia.

Phryne, as the slaves agreed and a painting of her shows, is an unusually beautiful girl. She is a Phrygian by birth and was sold into slavery by her parents, victims of extreme poverty. Ferox bought her a number of years ago, when she was fifteen. It is obvious from the way the slaves tell it that his purpose was purely sexual. She was virtually a prisoner in his room for months. However, while he was ill, Fabia made Phryne her personal *ornatrix*, dressed her in rich clothes and told her not to obey Ferox. When the senator recovered, he was not able to reclaim her, though he still legally owns her. Why he could sell Croesus, but not Phryne, I do not know, but the slaves said that there were many arguments between Ferox and Fabia over the slave girl. Ferox apparently just lost.

Prefect, the causes and exact nature of the enmity between the senator and his wife may ultimately be hidden deep within themselves. Perhaps Ferox felt the disappointment of his early passion for Fabia, while she may have felt the wounds of his rough and brutal character. Perhaps it stemmed from the affair with Anaximander many years ago in Ephesus or from their failure to have children, or from a combination of a hundred different things which go into making us what we are. But whatever it may be, Prefect, I am sure you will agree that the senator must be a prime target in my investigation.

Though your friendship with him makes such thoughts unseemly, it is entirely possible that Ferox is a murderer.

I have therefore made arrangements to visit the senator at his villa the day after tomorrow. I would go tomorrow. Prefect, but I would like to know the answers to several questions before I confront him. In particular, I want to trace the movements of Anaximander in Rome — where he lived, how long he'd been here, *et cetera*.

Though I have no leads. I can make reasonable assumptions and act on them. So I have assumed, Prefect, that Anaximander arrived in Rome recently, and that perhaps the fisherman and queen message-tablet sent to Fabia was one of his first acts on arriving. I will therefore try to find when and where he arrived and track him from there. Since Anaximander is from Ephesus, a ship is a most likely starting point, and I am sending one of my staff to the port tomorrow morning to see what he can learn.

It is also necessary to investigate others who might have motive to kill Fabia's past. and possibly present, lover. Her other lovers are natural suspects. The unfortunate slave Croesus, as I have said, was one of them. He was supposed to be sold to a farm chain gang a year ago. so the records of the slave trader to whom Ferox sold him may produce some further leads.

I will also try to trace the soldier Metellus and the philosopher Timotheus, both of whom were also named by Menelaus as having had affairs with Fabia. If Metellus is still with the Legion I Minervia in Germany. I must. of course, await an exchange of correspondence with him, though his presence there compels his innocence of any crime here in Rome.

But Timotheus may be more accessible. I have learned from the slaves that he is the senator's private tutor in Stoicism and perhaps his only confidante. That Fabia should count him among her lovers is, you will agree, somewhat sinister, but then, I suppose, not so surprising in view of what I have learned about Fabia and Ferox. Timotheus, the slaves said, lives somewhere in the Subura. While that overcrowded and active section of the City has successfully hidden numerous people who did not want to be found, there is no reason to believe that Timotheus is one of them.

Finally, Prefect, there is the matter of Fabia's former lover, Publius Planta. While his unfortunate fall from a balcony prevents belated revenge against his replacement, the ill-fated death of another of Fabia's lovers naturally arouses interest and suspicion.

I will keep you informed.

Vale.

/Seal/ Marcus Flavius Severus

THREE DAYS BEFORE THE IDES

VIII

VULSO VISITS THE PORT OF ROME

At the first hour, as dawn was breaking over the City, Vulso hailed a litter at the square near his apartment house and told the bearers to take him to the Ostia road gate in the old wall. He wore his centurion's uniform complete with medals and decorations, nine circular discs embossed with heads of animals and deities. They were fastened on a holder of leather straps and fitted over his leather cuirass, across his chest and abdomen. The top middle medallion bore the head of Medusa to ward off evil.

Vulso usually would have walked to the Ostia gate and if he rode he would have taken a sedan chair. Today, however, he hailed a large and sumptuous eight-bearer *lectica*. The government was paying the expenses of this trip and Vulso was going to ride in style.

At the posting station outside the gate, Vulso bought a seat on a comfortable four-horse, four-wheeled covered coach and rode the *Via Ostiensis* to the coast. The ride was refreshing after yesterday's long day in court. The country air was much cleaner and smelled much fresher than the sooty and often foul atmosphere in the City. The cool pine trees flanking the road, the grass and open fields, the monuments and villas visible from the highway were far more picturesque than a courtroom. The scenery was marred only by the placards that were beginning to go up on the tombs, trees and monuments announcing the chariot races scheduled for the Ides.

Vulso was on his way to Ostia, the seaport of Rome, with instructions from Judge Severus to backtrack Anaximander. It was Severus' surmise that Anaximander might not have been in Rome very long before he was murdered and the ship on which he travelled could still be in port. If so, perhaps the captain or one of the crew might remember him.

The centurion relaxed in his seat, stroked his swagger stick, and passed the time thinking about his two favorite subjects: war and women. After a while he thought about the case. To him, it was just another murder in a city glutted with them. But he knew how to solve it. All you had to do was to find someone who knew something and then pressure him into talking. It didn't matter what form of pressure he used, as long as it worked, though Vulso preferred physical violence. That always got some results and was certainly the quickest way. Judge Severus disagreed with him on that score, but he was a civilian and didn't correctly understand these matters. The judge reflected a modern Rome, enfeebled by Greeks, oriental cults and slaves. Vulso recalled a discussion with the judge just the other day about an item in the Daily Acts. Severus had praised the Athenian philosopher Demonax who, it had been reported, led a protest to prevent the introduction of gladiatorial games into Athens. Vulso had argued the games were beneficial, that they inured a soldier-race to blood and death and developed ideals of courage and glory. He had even cited Cicero and Pliny the Younger to the effect that the games taught the populace how to scorn wounds and face pain, while inculcating valor. Straton joined the discussion and made no secret that he resented Vulso's attitude and accused him of being cruel and barbaric. But there was more to it than that. Vulso had educated himself and had carefully considered the words of the philosophers who advocated such things as leniency and detachment. He simply disagreed with them. Life was too uncertain, too violent itself, to confront it with philosophic calm. What good would that do when the enemy was upon you? It was better to take the initiative and attack, full out, as you were taught in the Roman army. Let the others cave in first. And for that it was useful to open your eyes to the worst in men. Watching the Spectacles in the arena was a lesson in life. Underneath, Vulso suspected, the judge understood that, despite his praise of the Athenian trouble-maker. Else why did Severus employ him and in certain cases look the other way while Vulso employed his favorite methods? The centurion smiled cynically to himself and stroked his swagger stick again, as the city of Ostia came into view.

At the gate to the port city, Vulso hailed another eight-bearer litter, since Ostia, like Rome, prohibited wheeled traffic and horses on the streets during the day. Vulso was carried the length of the main street, the *Decumunas Maximus*, to the Ostia harbor complex which, when he arrived, was already alive with activity.

"The Port," as Ostia was familiarly called, was actually two harbors; an outer one built by the emperor Claudius and, connected to it by a narrow channel, an inner hexagonal harbor built more recently by the emperor Trajan. From the outer harbor, man-made moles curved out into the sea, framing an entrance 600 feet wide and a third of a mile square. Along the inside were quays and mooring docks with warehouses and other port facilities for servicing the far-flung merchant shipping of the empire. Rising high above the outer mole was a tall massive lighthouse. At night, the light of an intense fire would be reflected far out to sea by its huge convex mirror. An army of slave-stevedores milled about ships busily unloading wares, sometimes by hand, sometimes with the aid of huge derricks or 'storks', as they were called, set on revolving platforms which turned the mechanical hoists from dock to ship and back again. Teams of divers stood ready to leap into the water to retrieve fallen cargo, while an army of clerks scribbled away.

Vulso approached a clerk who sat on a stool recording in a ledger the unloading of a small cargo vessel. "I'm looking for a ship from Ephesus. One that may have arrived within the past two weeks."

"This isn't it," answered the clerk abruptly. "Ask at the port director's office." He tilted his head without lifting his eyes from the ledger. "Over there." Vulso walked to a portico, entered a room inside the colonnade and asked again. The information came fast and to the point. "That will be the *Asklepios* you want – cargo of onyx. It's in the inner harbor."

Vulso was on his way to the inner harbor when his attention was attracted to a crowd of stevedores, clerks and sailors rushing to the quayside. Two sleek quadriremes of the Imperial Navy, each over 100 feet long and bearing the flags of the Misenum Fleet, had dropped their moorings, lifted anchors, and began a race out of the harbor. One, a single-banked galley with four men to each oar, pulled out to the drumming of a mallet, while the other, a double-banked quadrireme with two sailors to each oar, sprinted in time to the playing of a flute. The cheers and urgings of the officers and deck personnel on each warship could be heard over the water spurring the enlisted men plying the oars below deck to greater effort. The onlookers on shore hurriedly placed bets while the race was still in doubt, until the double-banked galley pulled well into the lead. Then the crowd broke up and Vulso strolled to the inner harbor.

He had no difficulty finding the *Asklepios*. It was moored near the channel which connected the inner harbor to the Tiber River, so that its heavy cargo could be loaded onto barges and floated directly to the docks in Rome's Aventine Region. The *Asklepios* was a two-masted merchantman, a medium-sized freighter about 100 feet long and 30 feet wide with a capacity of 300 tons. A statue of the god Asklepios was mounted on the stern identifying the ship. The sides were dramatically painted in dark blue wax, with decorative bands of red running its length. The steering oars were yellow and the large curved gooseneck stern post, the sign of merchant ships, was painted gold. A mechanical stork on the wharf was positioned over the ship's hold, while naked sailors on board were attaching slabs of onyx to the derrick. Vulso climbed the gangway and spoke to a deck officer.

"Is the *gubernator* on board?"

"Who wants him?" asked the tunic-clad officer.

"Court of the Urban Prefect," replied Vulso.

"Wait here," the sailor answered and walked aft to the large deckhouse. A few moments later he returned and motioned Vulso to follow him inside. He was led into one of the cabins where the captain was lying on a couch rubbing his eyes as if awakening.

"What does the prefect want with me?" asked the captain. "All I do is sail this ship. If there are any legal problems, go see the owner."

"I'm not interested in legal problems but in one of your passengers. You had passengers on this voyage, didn't you?"

"Certainly, centurion," acknowledged the captain. "About 200." He turned to the officer. "Get Theudis," he instructed. Then, to Vulso: "Theudis is the *toicharchos*, responsible for the cargo and the passengers.

While they were waiting Vulso asked about the details of the journey from Ephesus.

"We docked five days ago, eight days before the Ides." Vulso noted the date: it was the day before Fabia disappeared. "The weather was a little rough," the captain went on. "It's near the end of the sailing season for ships from the east to Rome. We had to ride out a storm at Pylos, in the bay of Sphacteria, on the west coast of Greece. It took us an extra week to make the run from Ephesus." He yawned. "Who is the passenger you want?"

"A mosaicist from Ephesus by the name of Anaximander."

"What do you want him for?" asked the captain casually.

"The prefect likes mosaics," obliged Vulso.

They waited in silence until the *toicharchos* entered the cabin.

"He's interested in a passenger named Anaximander, a mosaicist from Ephesus," said the captain in Greek. "Know him?"

The officer consulted a scroll with the ship's manifest. "I don't remember him," he said. "But his name's on the list, so he was on board. What about him?"

Vulso addressed the officer directly in Greek. "Court of the Urban Prefect. I want to know whatever you can find out about this Anaximander, whether any of the crew knew him, and especially where he went after he left the ship." He handed him the painting of Anaximander.

The captain instructed Theudis to talk to the crew, find out who knew him, and bring anyone who did into his cabin. Theudis reappeared a short while later followed by a wispy old man. "This is Hermaios, the ship's carpenter," he said, returning the painting to Vulso. "He knows Anaximander."

Vulso questioned the carpenter. "Where did you meet Anaximander? On board or in Ephesus?"

"On board," answered Hermaios. "We struck up a conversation early in the voyage. He said he was a mosaicist, but that carpentry was a hobby. We talked about carpentry."

"Did he say why he was going to Rome?"

"He said he was going to make his fortune. Not that things were bad in Ephesus. Since that earthquake about seven years ago there's been plenty of work and Anaximander said he had been working for a few years on the baths the emperor Antoninus Pius is having built. But he said he knew someone in Rome who would get him well paying jobs making mosaics for rich Romans. He said all his worries were over. He had a patron."

"Did he say who this patron was?"

"No. He only said it was someone he had known in Ephesus, a rich woman, a Roman. She sent for him, he said."

"Do you know where I can find him? It's very important."

Hermaios hesitated. "He didn't do anything wrong, did he?"

"Nothing like that," answered Vulso. "But one of the well-paying jobs he was to do was for the prefect and we haven't been able to find him."

"Oh," said the carpenter, "maybe I can help you. I told him we would probably winter in Ostia and that I intended to visit Rome and tour the city after the cargo was unloaded. He invited me to spend some time with him. We could talk about carpentry and see the sights together."

"Where were you to meet him?"

"He said he wasn't sure where he would live eventually. He hoped his patron would find him an apartment, but he said he was first going to a hotel near the Ostia gate called 'Athena's Mantle.' He said if he wasn't there when I came up to Rome, he would leave word there."

Vulso smiled pleasantly and went off to gorge himself on oysters at his favorite Ostia seafood restaurant.

IX

STRATON SEARCHES THE SUBURA AND RUNS INTO TROUBLE

Straton's feet were killing him. Dressed as a Greek philosopher of the Cynic School, with a rough woolen traveler's cloak, a walking stick and a wallet, the judge's aide had criss-crossed the Subura since early morning trying to find Ferox' philosopher, Timotheus. He had gone from one taverna to another, made the rounds of the cookshops, bookshops and antique stores, talked to local merchants and apartment house porters, asked water vendors, street corner poets, street musicians, dice players, beggars and even the idlers and loungers who spent their time leaning against walls and sitting on curbs. He had gotten nowhere. A few people had heard of Timotheus, some even knew him by sight, but no one knew or would tell him where he could be found. And now, by late morning, the clamor was beginning to get on Straton's nerves and he didn't feel like pushing his way through more crowds on more narrow streets.

He entered a large taverna with the signpost painting of a bull and a gladiator. Like many taverns, it had a bar facing the street to provide quick refreshment to those in a hurry. Behind the bar, the interior, larger than most, was more like a small hall, with a mezzanine making a second floor. The place was crowded and noisy with customers drinking and yakking and Spanish dancing girls gyrating the lively and obscene *cordax*, clicking their castanets to the musical accompaniment of lyres, flutes and tambourines. Straton collapsed on a stool and looked around.

On one wall hung a painting of the emperor, flanked by portraits of his two adopted sons and heirs, Marcus Aurelius and Lucius Verus. The other walls were decorated with crude, garish frescoes depicting bloody scenes from the arena. Straton noted that the frescoes featured a gladiator with the name Taurus, the Bull, written above his head. He was slaying one foe after another, like some hero of Greek mythology. Undoubtedly this Taurus owned the tavern, since many such establishments were run by former athletes, gladiators or charioteers, whose reputations drew customers. Fans were always interested in hearing inside stories of the circus or arena, not only out of sporting interest but also to get an edge for placing bets on forthcoming events. The crowd in Taurus' differed very little from the clientele in the other Subura taverns except perhaps in here the mood may have been more boisterous, the jokes cruder and the laughter more raucous.

Straton was sitting at a table already occupied by three men. They were studying the list of gladiators for the next games and trying to figure out which gladiators would be matched against each other in the forthcoming games, information never revealed until the fights began. The trio argued at the top of their lungs about whom to bet on if various hypothetical pairings took place.

Straton ordered *calda* from a slave-waiter – about his tenth cup of the day. So much cheap wine was making him uncomfortable; already he had stopped three times to use a public urinal or street corner jar to relieve himself. Now he listened in silent anger to the conversation, hating these lower class Romans. They lived off the State, regarding the dole as a sort of booty to which, as Romans, they were entitled by right of conquest and tradition, along with freedom from taxation. Every month they collected their food through the grain dole, avoided boredom thanks to some 135 yearly days of free public spectacles and supplemented their incomes by schemes ranging from petty frauds to robberies and murders.

Straton had heard there was an item in the Daily Acts the other day reporting that the emperor had taken away the salaries of some idlers in the imperial bureaucracy. "Nothing was more sordid, even crueler," the emperor said, "than gnawing away the public weal while conferring nothing back by their own labor." Yet, Straton thought, many of the 200,000 citizens on the public dole did exactly that and were encouraged in their indolence by official policy. But it was too late, he knew, to change that 300-year-old policy, for no emperor could survive the massive street rioting that would follow. The Roman mob was discordant and seditious and uncontrollable, which was why the State provided the bread and circuses in the first place.

"What do you say, philosopher?" one of the men at the table asked in bad Greek. "Suppose the net and trident man Astianax is matched with the light-armed swordsman Fortunatus. Who will win?"

"Fortunatus will lose," answered Straton in Latin, saying the first thing that came to his mind.

"See," said the questioner to his companions, "the philosopher agrees with me. I have the support of philosophy."

"That's what you think, cabbage head!" sneered one of his cronies. "Whatever a philosopher says, I do the opposite. My money is with Fortunatus, provided he fights with Astianax. Now if he fights with the net and trident man Saturninus, that's another story." The three began arguing among themselves again, with the words "shit," "asshole" and "fuck" featuring prominently in their analysis.

The slave-waiter brought Straton's *calda* and in a low voice asked him if he was the one making inquiries in the Subura about Timotheus.

"Why, yes," answered Straton in surprise.

"Then Taurus would like to speak to you – upstairs." He motioned to the rear of the tavern.

Straton left his *calda* on the table and walked up the steps, pleased that word had gotten around and that he finally might be onto a lead. A slave on the second-floor landing directed him to a room on the left. As soon as he was inside, the door was slammed shut, strong hands grabbed him by the shoulders and threw him on the floor.

"What is this?" said Straton, looking up at three men standing above him. "What did you do that for?"

"Who are you?" asked one of the men with a bull's neck, a cow's face, and muscles that stretched his tunic. Straton took him for the gladiator Taurus.

"I'm a friend of Timotheus. My name is Straton."

"Timotheus says he doesn't know you. Now, who are you?" repeated Taurus, landing a kick in Straton's shin for emphasis.

Straton winced. "It's true, but Senator Lucius Junius Ferox, who Timotheus does know, told me to look him up."

As Straton stressed the word 'senator', the men looked at each other. "When did he tell you this?" asked the gladiator suspiciously.

"A few days ago, the seventh day before the Ides," improvised Straton. "At his villa outside the City."

"We'll see." He motioned to one of the men who left the room.

"Can I get up?" said Straton.

"Stay where you are or I'll break you in two!"

Straton braced his back against the wall and sat on the floor. "How do you know Timotheus?" he asked the gladiator. "Are you studying philosophy with him?"

"Very funny," said Taurus.

Straton tried again. "Senator Ferox won't be too pleased at the way I'm being treated. I'm his favorite philosopher."

"I hope for your sake you're not. Timotheus doesn't like competition."

Just then the door opened and the man who had left the room returned and whispered into Taurus' ear.

"Timotheus says he was with Ferox at his villa on the seventh day before the Ides and you weren't." The gladiator smiled. Then he picked Straton up and drove his fist into his face.

X

SEVERUS HIRES AN ASSESSOR AND QUESTIONS A PRAETORIAN

Judge Severus was feeling frustrated. It was already midday and neither of the two witnesses he summoned had arrived. Squilla, the slave dealer to whom the slave Croesus had been sold, was supposed to be there with his records. At least Severus had sent court slaves with a subpoena to bring in Squilla and his books. Perhaps they had trouble locating him, perhaps he was not even in Rome, but away on a business trip. And Metellus, the soldier who had an affair with Fabia, he should have been there also. A check of the army records had shown that while there was no Sextus Anicius Metellus with the I Minervia Legion in Germany, there was someone by that name in the Praetorian Guard in Rome. A subpoena for his production had been served on the Praetorian Prefect in the morning. Why wasn't Metellus there yet?

After a short court session the judge occupied his morning by interviewing candidates for a job as his law assistant and permanent judicial assessor. Four young men were there applying for the position. Each of the candidates had Equestrian status; otherwise they were quite different.

The first had studied advocacy under the famous rhetorician Titus Castricius and quoted his teacher's creed that in representing a client "a lawyer is permitted to make statements that are false, reckless, tricky, underhanded and deceptive, provided they have some similarity to the truth and can cleverly insinuate themselves into the minds of those to be influenced." The candidate seemed as slimy as his mentor and Severus didn't like him at all. Besides, he wore a ring on every finger – a total disqualification in the judge's mind.

The second candidate said all the things a judge ordinarily wanted to hear and in the way a judge ordinarily wanted to hear them: The "art of Rome" – here he was echoing Vergil – was to "ordain peace with law," the most noble calling for a man was a career in public service, etc. Severus didn't quite know whether the young man believed what he said or whether he was faking it. In either case he overdid it. Thus, expounding the merits of the various jurists who sat on the emperor's *consilium*, the candidate proclaimed that he was "looking forward to reading the 16-volume work on Trusts by Volusius Maecianus, one of the great legal scholars in the *consilium*, though, of course, by no means the most prolific or illustrious."

The third candidate had experience. He had practiced as an *advocatus fisci*, a lawyer for the Bureau of the Treasury who toured the provinces prosecut-

ing cases of tax evasion and delinquency. He spoke
convincingly about the importance of the job he had.
Despite the fact that there was peace and prosperity in
the empire and that personal income had gone up, the
State, he said, was always on the brink of bankruptcy.
Few people, he argued, understood the cost of running
the empire. Huge sums were spent on public welfare
and education, on disaster relief and public works, not
to mention military expenditures. Too many provin-
cials were becoming Roman citizens, thereby reducing
the tax base. Where was the money to come from,
he asked. Only effective tax collection enabled the
empire to function properly.

Severus was not interested in taxes and dismissed the
applicant with a wave.

The fourth candidate was hired. Gaius Sempronius
Flaccus had studied law at the school of Sabinus and
Cassius, not only the best law school in Rome, but also
the same one Severus and his family had attended for
three generations. Flaccus told the judge breezily that
he wanted to make a lot of money and become a prefect.
Severus thought he better test him with a legal problem
and asked him to consider a situation that had troubled
his friend, Aulus Gellius, when presiding as a judge in
the Court of the Praetor. Gellius had to decide a case
where an honest person claimed, but without proof, that
a dishonest man owed him money, and the dishonest man
denied it. People had given different advice when Gellius sought it — a philosopher, that the honest man should
win; lawyers, that the dishonest man should — "after all,
there was no proof," they argued — until the judge took

an oath that the matter was unclear to him and stepped out of the case.

"The judge is too much the philosopher to find for the defendant and too much the lawyer to find for the plaintiff," commented Flaccus. "In his place I would realize I was dealing with a legal problem and not a philosophical one, so the solution would be easy."

Severus looked at him inquiringly.

"The rescript of the emperor Hadrian to Vibius Varro, proconsul of Cilicia, says the judge should decide who's telling the truth and who's lying by taking into consideration who the witnesses are, their status in society, their reputation, how they act when testifying, how they answer questions, etc. If a judge can't make that decision, then he must apply the law which states that 'the burden of proof is on the plaintiff and not on the defendant.' So since the honest man – the plaintiff – did not meet his burden of proof, the judge should dismiss the case and find for the dishonest man," he concluded with a flourish. "It is his legal duty."

Severus laughed, but pointed out that when a judge walks out of a case and refuses to interpret the law in favor of a dishonest man, he fulfills a moral duty in addition to a legal one. "Deciding a case 'according to the laws' must be interpreted as 'according to the spirit of the laws' as well as 'according to the letter of the laws,' as one of our jurisconsults has said."

Severus sized Flaccus up with a shrewd look and decided to hire him. "If you'd like to start as my assessor immediately, I have something interesting for you."

All smiles, the young man assented eagerly.

"We're looking for a woman who has disappeared," explained the judge. "I've been told that there was a man who knew her well, an admirer, a lover. Unfortunately, he died a few years ago. He fell off a balcony, it seems. I'd like to talk to someone who knew him well. A surviving family member or close friend. Perhaps, Flaccus, you could find that someone for me."

"Where do I start?"

"The man's name was Publius Planta. He was a member of the Senatorial class. Try the files of the Daily Acts. Planta's death must have been in the news. It was about two years ago."

"When do you want it by?" said Flaccus with alacrity.

"As soon as possible."

Severus filled his new assessor in more carefully on the details of the case. As he was about to go and introduce him to the court staff, Proculus met them at the door.

"The Praetorian Metellus is here," reported the clerk.

"Show him in," replied the judge.

Metellus wore the civilian dress of a Roman citizen, white tunic and toga, required of guardsmen on duty at the palace. The first emperor, Augustus, set the policy 150 years before and it was followed by every emperor since. The trappings of the regime should display the trappings of the Republic, whatever the reality. As *princeps* – first citizen – no emperor should be seen surrounded by soldiers, only by civilians. Otherwise it would irk the sensitivities of the Roman people. So the emperor's personal bodyguard must carry sword and dagger concealed underneath a toga, and only wear military uniforms in the barracks, on the street, on campaign, and for seducing women.

Metellus was a tall, handsome, young man with a swarthy complexion and deep set brown eyes. He stood at attention, but seemed nervous in the presence of the judge. He didn't know why he had been subpoenaed.

Severus sat on a comfortable camp chair and directed the soldier to a similar chair facing him. He began in a relaxed manner.

"There's some information I need from you, information I realize you might be reluctant to discuss with me. But I can assure you I will keep your answers confidential, unless forced to do otherwise, and if they are full and honest I will commend your cooperation to the Praetorian Prefect. If not..." Severus made a motion with open upturned palm and left the sentence hang.

"I'll try to help, *eminentissime*," Metellus replied, still unsure of why he was there. "What is it you want to know?"

"Everything you know about Fabia, the wife of Senator Ferox, with particular emphasis on your love affair with her."

Metellus relaxed and smiled. "This is not a problem, judge. She's nothing to me and she never was. It's true that I went to bed with her. But so what. She's not the only woman in Rome who swings a loose hip."

"Start at the beginning," interrupted Severus. "When did you meet her, and where?"

"Senator Ferox is an old friend of my father's. When I was with the legion in Germany I was sent to Rome as part of an escort for one of the legionary tribunes who had business here. This was about a year ago. On the way I stopped at home, in Ravenna, to visit my family. They suspected that I intended to live in the brothels while in Rome, so they arranged for me to stay at the house of Senator Ferox." He laughed. "They were right. Staying there did keep me out of the brothels. His wife pounced on me the first night I was there. Really, judge, it's true. I noticed her eyeing me the moment I arrived, and at dinner that night she began playing up to me. I can't say I wasn't interested, but I was tired from the trip and went to bed early. Then in the middle of the night I felt a woman arousing me. I didn't even know who she was until afterwards. From then on, every time I came back at night from making the rounds of the Subura taverns, she would be waiting for me in my bed. I even tried to get her to be more secretive about it. After all, her husband was living in the house. The slaves knew about it. I could tell by the way they smirked at me when they thought I wasn't looking. But she was brazen about it. She said she would take care of her husband."

"Have you seen her since you became a Praetorian and returned to Rome?"

"No. I had enough of her. In a way I was even glad, after a month of staying at her house, that I had to go back to the legion. She was becoming a nuisance by then. She thought she owned me. She doesn't know I'm here and that's the way I like it. I don't want her chasing me around Rome. Besides, your honor, in my uniform I can get practically any girl in Rome I want."

"Did the senator ever let on that he knew about your affair with his wife? How did he treat you, for instance?"

"He avoided me, but when he couldn't, he was polite. He was always in the company of some philosopher type.

I would usually see them discussing things in whispered conversations. This philosopher seemed to be toadying up to the senator, always complimenting him in public. He sometimes laid it on a bit thick, I thought. A fortune hunter, in my opinion, waiting for Ferox to die and leave him money in his will. But Ferox didn't seem to mind at all. He would drag this philosopher around with him wherever he went."

"Do you remember the philosopher's name?"

"Some Greek name or other, Dorotheus, Theophilus..."

"Timotheus?" suggested Severus.

"That was it. I didn't like him much. He was always glaring at me and asking stupid questions like, if one grain at a time were taken away from a heap, when would it cease to be a heap. I thought he was trying to degrade me, make me appear to be an idiot. I finally took him aside one day and told him I was going to take that philosopher's cane of his and shove it up his ass." He laughed. "He kept out of my way after that."

"Do you remember Fabia's personal slave, Phryne?"

"Now there's a girl I would like to poke. I haven't seen many better looking than her. Fabia isn't bad, but Phryne, she could really arouse a man." He paused. "But I think Fabia and Phryne were sleeping together."

Severus raised his eyebrows. "What makes you think that?"

"From things Fabia said — I don't remember specifically — hints, you know. Fabia was always petting her, for instance, fondling her, often when Ferox was around. She would say to Ferox, 'doesn't Phryne look beautiful today' or something along those lines, and then run her hand over her behind or on her breasts. Then Fabia once saw me looking at Phryne the way man looks at a woman like her, and told me that night not to get any ideas into my head. Phryne, she said, belonged to her. And she laughed in such a way that I suspected what I just told you, that Fabia and Phryne were sleeping together."

"How did Phryne react to this?" asked the judge with interest. "I mean to being fondled by Fabia in Ferox' presence."

"There was nothing she could do about it. She was a slave, after all. She had to submit. But she didn't like it, that's for sure."

"How do you know?"

"One time I was idly sitting by the fish pond in the peristyle when I saw Fabia and Phryne come from one direction in the house and Ferox from another. Their paths crossed on the other side of the pool, and Fabia stopped and began to fondle Phryne and taunt Ferox in the way I said. I don't know whether they saw me or didn't care whether I saw them, but there was no mistaking what happened. Fabia lingered over Phryne's body. Then, afterwards, Phryne began to cry. Fabia told her to stop sniveling and when Phryne wouldn't, or couldn't, Fabia slapped her in the face. Hard. A few other slaves busy cleaning in the area stopped and stared at the sound of it. But the slap made Phryne cry even more. Then Fabia screamed at her, something about if she wanted to wet her face, there was a better way than tears, and then pushed her right into the fish pond. Fabia stalked away and some of the other slaves went into the water and pulled Phryne out."

"And Ferox? How did he take all this?"

"There was murder in his eyes."

Severus became thoughtful for a few moments and then continued the questioning. "Do you remember a slave named Croesus?"

"Do you know why he was called Croesus?" countered Metellus in response.

"No," said the judge, interested. "Why?"

"Fabia once told me. It was at dinner one night. Ferox was there, so was that worm Timotheus. Croesus, she told me, was the King of Lydia, the richest man who ever lived. So why, she said, did I think she named this poor slave Croesus? What wealth did he have? I said I didn't know. So she ordered Croesus to take off his clothes, right there in front of everyone. I saw immediately in what way he was richly endowed. Fabia broke out laughing. She said that Ferox wanted to name him Cato, since he had some smattering of philosophy."

"What did Ferox say to that, do you remember?"

"I remember it perfectly because it struck me as odd. Ferox just glared at her and said, 'are you prepared to play Apollo to my Cyrus.'"

"Did you understand the allusion?"

"Not then. But I was curious, so I asked around. A friend later explained it to me."

"Yes," said Severus. "King Croesus was defeated by Cyrus, the King of Persia and sentenced to be burned at the stake. Later Cyrus relented, but it was too late. Nothing could be done, the fire had been lit. But the god Apollo interceded and caused a violent rainstorm to put out the flames. Apparently Ferox was preparing to 'burn' Croesus and daring Fabia to put out the flames." He eyed the Praetorian. "Where were you four days ago, the seventh day before the Ides? I want you to account for your time from then until now."

Metellus' voice was firm. "I've been on duty every day for the past two weeks, judge. During the day I'm on the Palatine Hill and at night it's the barracks. The last four days were no exception. You can ask my centurion."

The judge rose from his couch and told Metellus he could go. "I may call on you again. But you've been forthcoming and helpful and I will mention your cooperation to your prefect."

Metellus saluted and left. The judge summoned Proculus and asked if the slave dealer Squilla had arrived yet.

"No, judge. He wasn't at the market this morning, but he should be back in the next hour for an auction. I was just about to send the court-slaves out again."

Severus spied Alexander sitting in the clerk's office, reading documents of old legal cases. He told Proculus not to send anyone and ambled over to his own slave. "Alexander, I'm going to the slave market to question a witness. Come with me."

Alexander looked puzzled, as if to say 'why me?'. But he silently put his reading aside and followed the judge.

XI

SEVERUS AND ALEXANDER GO TO THE SLAVE MARKET

Severus and Alexander waited at the back of the crowd in the slave market, while the slave-dealer Squilla was informed that a Roman judge had come to see him on official business. Meanwhile they watched the buyers inspect the merchandise as the auction time neared.

The slaves were old and young, men and women, girls and boys, from all over the empire and beyond: Northerners valued for the stature and strength, black Africans for their exotic appearance, Asians for their astuteness and submissiveness, Greeks for their culture and culinary arts, youths for their sexual appeal. Most were confined in small slave pens where notices, chalked in red on white boards, recited information about the occupant. Others stood on the display line, their feet chalked white to show they were for immediate sale. Interested customers were busy examining the 'speaking tools,' testing muscles, gripping teeth, poking and prodding, stroking and fondling. Always they lifted the single garment worn by the slave, for hadn't Seneca observed, "when you buy a horse, you order its blanket to be removed; so, too, you pull the garments off a slave." Some buyers had physicians along to check more closely for health and disease, while others questioned clerks about the propensity and personality of the tool they were considering. Others spoke directly to the slave, ferreting out his command of language and learning or lack of it. Some conducted their examination gently, some roughly; some were humane, others degenerate. The random misfortunes that had brought the slaves to this place were ameliorated or compounded by who they attracted. Some viewed the customers with relief, others with fear. Because the chattel knew what was happening, it was worse than the cattle market.

The bell rang. The crowd turned its attention to a beautiful teen-age girl led from the head of the display line to a rotating platform. She was stripped and slowly revolved, while the auctioneer began his patter, extoling her teeth and legs, her clear skin and luscious figure. She had some training as a hairdresser and a smattering of Greek learning, he proclaimed, and she could also sing at dinner parties. "You'll wait a long time for another bargain like her," he concluded and offered the girl at 20,000 sesterces. A woman, whose coiffure looked like it could benefit from a new hairdresser, opened the bidding at 20,000. A second buyer, an old man with no hair, bid 25,000.

Alexander's face was ashen. He remembered a time when, as a child, he had been sold in just such a manner. But he spoke to Severus diplomatically. "*Kyrie*, I know that I am treated like a member of your family and that perhaps my status as a slave is one of form more than substance since I'm even paid a good salary. But seeing a scene like this impresses upon me the truth of the definition of slavery in Roman law; that it is an institution of the Law of Nations which is contrary to Nature. Does it not impress you the same way?"

"It does."

"And if Nature is morally greater than any law of nations, as philosophers universally agree, then does it not lead you to certain conclusions regarding the way in which society should be constructed?"

"Yes, Alexander, in theory. But the fact that slavery is universal among all nations reflects its necessity in society. As Aristotle says, 'if every tool could, at the word of command, go to work by itself, if the looms wove untended, and a plectrum could play the lyre of its own accord, then employers would dispense with workers and masters dismiss their slaves.' But that day has not arrived. Perhaps if the god Hephaestus came to Earth with the automata Homer writes about, with his tripods on wheels which move by themselves or his metal handmaidens who attend his needs or the bellows of his forge which work spontaneously on command, then the laws of nations could more easily be in accord with Nature."

"But, *kyrie*, even if nations are unable to guide themselves to be in tune with Nature, cannot we as individuals conform our conduct and our lives to follow Nature? Isn't living in accordance with Nature the highest good in Platonism, in Stoicism, in Epicureanism, and in most schools of philosophy?"

Severus caught the implication. "We are all slaves, Alexander, whether to a person or a passion or to whatever it is that compels us to do what we do. To quote Seneca, 'we are fellow slaves, if you realize that Fortune has the same sway over everyone.'"

Alexander shook his head in exasperation and gave his master a dirty look. "That may be true, *kyrie*, but it is not a sufficient answer to my question." Severus noted the look as well as a certain bitterness in Alexander's tone of voice.

"Please come this way, *eminentissime*," interrupted Squilla's slave, and led them behind the auctioneer's platform. The woman had just bid 30,000 sesterces. The bald man countered with 35.

They were shown through a clerk's office filled with busy men recording data, at least when they weren't bowing in deference to the passage of a Roman magistrate. Squilla received Severus and Alexander at the entrance to his private office, but didn't dare attempt a greeting kiss. His status and profession were too low for a Roman judge to tolerate the familiarity. Squilla was a thin, wiry old man, whose pinched cheeks, sharp eyes and unhealthy pallor betrayed a shrewdness that engendered mistrust. He was nervous as well. Visits from the law usually meant bad news for a slave trader and Squilla suspected the worst.

"I'm here to inquire about the sale to you of a slave of Senator Lucius Junius Ferox," said Severus as he settled himself on a couch and waived away proffered wine and sweets. "The slave's name is Croesus. You purchased him from the senator about a year ago."

"I will check the records, *eminentissime*." Squilla ran to the door and shouted orders into the clerk's office.

He returned to stand in front of the judge. Severus glared at him without saying a word, waiting for the records to be brought. After several minutes the tension got to the slave dealer. "I'll get them myself, *eminentissime*." He hurried to the door again. "Those incompetents," he muttered. A short burst of screaming and yelling issued from the office and Squilla rushed back with two rolled sheets of papyrus. He untied the strings and handed them to the judge.

Severus read the documents and then handed them to Alexander, standing next to the couch. "One is a bill of sale from Ferox to Squilla. The second is another bill of sale, executed the very next day, recording the sale of Croesus from Squilla to Fabia." He faced the slave trader. "The slave Croesus wasn't here too long, was he Squilla. Tell me what you know about this."

"I recall the transaction...both transactions, *eminentissime*. I handled them myself. Senator Ferox came to me with this slave all bound up, saying he wanted him sold to a chain gang."

"But you sold him to Ferox' wife the next day, not to a chain gang, and for a healthy profit too."

"She implored me. What could I do but to give in to such a revered lady."

"What did you tell Ferox about the resale?"

"Nothing, *eminentissime*. He has not been back since. I have not seen him in the last year."

"Why did Ferox pick you to sell the slave Croesus to?"

"I do not know *eminentissime*."

"Had you sold Ferox any slaves in the past?"

"Not to my knowledge. I had never seen the senator before."

"Perhaps, then, you have a reputation for slave trading with chain gangs, is that why?"

Squilla squirmed. "May the gods be witness that my reputation is only of the highest. You have merely to watch how considerately I conduct my auctions to know how I am thought of. Besides, corporations that use chain gangs, in the mines or on farms or elsewhere, have every right to purchase whatever slaves they want. It violates no law."

"Then there is nothing else you can tell me about Senator Ferox or Fabia?"

"Nothing, *eminentissime*. I have had no contact with either of them, before those transactions or since."

Severus and Alexander left by the way they entered. A young boy was now on the revolving platform and the bidding was active.

"If Fabia bought back Croesus a year ago and he is not at the Ferox mansion, where is he?" asked Alexander. "And more importantly, where was he when Anaximander arrived in Rome?"

"I'm wondering about that too. Where has Croesus been for the past year? Fabia must have kept him somewhere. But where?"

They walked briskly out of the slave market and then strolled more leisurely in the direction of the judge's chambers.

"If Croesus was Fabia's lover," commented Alexander, "and a new lover arrived on the scene, that might give him a powerful motive for getting rid of Anaximander. Besides, Croesus was now Fabia's slave as well. And you know the saying," he added with only the slightest touch of irony, "so many slaves, so many enemies."

XII

VULSO FINDS THE ATHENA'S MANTLE HOTEL

Vulso was back in Rome by early afternoon. He found the hotel "Athena's Mantle" on a side street off Public Swimming Pool Street, not far from the Ostia gate. It was next door to a brothel, as the wall graffiti indicated. Vulso stopped to read them:

Arphocras had all he wanted here with Drauca for a denarius.

Whoever comes here, read this before he does anything else: if he wants a good time, remember Attice charges only 4 sesterces.

No man is handsome unless he loves a woman.

Whoever loves is faring well.

Whoever loves is lost.

The hotel looked as if its beds were stuffed with reeds rather than goose feathers, but Vulso had seen much worse. There was a small restaurant on the ground floor, with the rooms upstairs. Two female slaves were busy cleaning when Vulso entered. A portrait of the emperor hung near the entrance and lewd frescoes of satyrs chasing nymphs decorated the walls. A placard advertised the hotel with the common formula — "Service after the Roman fashion and standard."

"Where is the owner?" Vulso called out.

A small thin man, his hands clasped together, appeared as if out of nowhere. Bending over in an obsequious manner, he asked if he might be of service. "I am Papnoutis, the proprietor. You can have a room a meal and a girl, all for only 75 sesterces. And," he added with a touch of pride, "you can be sure that any girl you have at Athena's Mantle is registered on the rolls of the City Aedile."

The proprietor's name was Egyptian. Vulso took a moment to size him up and decide how to handle him.

"Court of the Urban Prefect," he said crisply. "You're under arrest." He grabbed Papnoutis by the arm and dragged him toward the door. Taken completely aback, the man alternated gurgles and screams. "I didn't do anything! What did I do? Someone help me!"

Vulso threw him against the wall. "You didn't report that Anaximander stayed here."

"Who is Anaximander? Who am I supposed to report to?" said Papnoutis frantically.

Vulso slapped him in the face. He pulled out the papyrus with the painting of Anaximander. "This is Anaximander."

"I don't know him, I..."

Vulso slapped him harder.

"Wait. Stop. He stayed here. I didn't know I should report him. Don't hit me. He came five days ago, on the eighth day before the Ides."

"Where is his room?"

"Upstairs. I'll show you. But he's not here. He stayed only one night. He went out the next day and didn't return."

"Show me," said Vulso, pushing Papnoutis toward the stairs with his swagger stick.

The proprietor led him to a room on the second floor. On these walls, Vulso noticed, the nymphs were chasing the satyrs. Presumably, he thought, they would catch each other on the third floor walls. Papnoutis selected a key from the ring which hung on his tunic belt and opened the door.

"You see, he's not here," he said, a little calmer now, but still shaken.

"Wait outside and close the door. And don't go downstairs or speak to anyone."

Papnoutis followed instructions and Vulso searched the room. It contained a bed, a stool and a table. Nothing was in plain view, so he ripped open the bedding. Nothing there either. Just reeds. Vulso went to the door and called Papnoutis back in. "Where are his belongings?"

"Downstairs. I was keeping them for him until he returned."

"Let me see."

They went downstairs to a room which served as an office. Vulso was handed a traveler's musette bag with a leather shoulder strap. "There's only clothes and scrolls and a few tablets. I didn't touch anything."

Vulso rummaged the contents, closed the bag and said he was taking it with him. "Now, I want to know if he had any visitors."

"Just one. A woman. He arrived on the eighth day before the Ides and left with her in the afternoon of the seventh." The seventh, Vulso noted, was the day Fabia disappeared and two days before Anaximander's body was found on the steps of the Temple of Mars the Avenger. He showed Papnoutis the painting of Fabia. "This one?"

"No, it wasn't her. I would remember. She was also very good looking, but had blonde hair."

Vulso unrolled the painting of Phryne.

"That looks like her. She came in the late afternoon. She asked for Anaximander and went to his room. They left together a few minutes later."

"Which way did they go?"

"I don't know. Towards the center of the city, I think. I didn't watch them."

"Since you've been cooperative," said Vulso, "I've changed my mind about arresting you. But if anyone comes to inquire about Anaximander, you had better let me know. Just report it to the *Vigiles* precinct in this Region of the City."

Papnoutis mopped his brow with his arm and let out a sigh of relief. Smiling broadly, Vulso left with Anaximander's belongings. He hailed a litter and told the bearers to take him to the Forum of Augustus. He was heading directly back to Judge Severus' chambers.

XIII

FABIA'S LOVE LETTERS

Daylight was ebbing away. A light rain fell on Rome for the third afternoon in a row. Judge Severus reclined on his office reading couch, absorbed in Lucius Apuleius' entertaining account of his defense in a provincial court against a charge of magic. The book was the rage of Rome's legal world, a trial record, yet a sophisticated satire of outmoded notions still rampant outside Rome. Some of Apuleius' big-city ways, like using tooth powder, had been cited in court by his accusers as evidence of spell casting, a charge with which the witty lawyer had particularly amused the judges and his readers. Severus read the book with a merry grin.

The rain continued to beat against the shutters, now and then whipped up by a brisk wind. There was a knock on the door. Severus looked up from his book to see Vulso striding across the room, a travel bag slung over his shoulders.

"How was it today, Vulso?" asked the judge with a touch of sarcasm. "All eight-bearer litters and a big meal as usual?"

Vulso laughed. "Of course. But at least when I charge the State for litter rides and a big meal, it's honest. Not like a lot of people who actually walk and eat only snacks." He opened the bag and dumped the contents on the table in front of Severus' couch. "These are Anaximander's," he announced.

"Good work!" exclaimed Severus, rolling up his book scroll and putting it aside. "How and where did you find it?"

Vulso told him and then asked about Straton. "Did he find Timotheus?"

"I haven't heard from him yet. Pull up a stool and let's see what's here."

They examined the contents of the bag. The tablets, they both noted mentally, were fashionably small 'Vitellian Tablets', used commonly for intimate personal messages and love letters. Severus glanced at a few scrolls. They were books, one on mosaics, a book of poems, another of love epigrams by Callimachus. Vulso opened the crossed threads on the first tablet he picked up, noticing the seal had already been broken. "It's a letter," he said. "And guess who wrote it?"

"From Fabia to Anaximander," read Severus, looking at a second tablet.

There were five in all. The threads on some were worn thin, as if they had been opened and closed many times.

"Love letters," went on the judge scanning the contents. "Vulso, check if they're dated. This one isn't."

"Neither is this," said Vulso.

"None of them are," rejoined Severus, as he opened another and looked inside. He turned on his side, placed a tablet on the couch and began to read aloud in Greek.

Fabia to my sweetest and most honored fisherman, Anaximander, very many greetings:

I rejoiced greatly at receiving your letter which was given to me by the mime player.

I wish you to be happy always, as I wish it for myself, but I grieve that you are away from me.

Be patient. Our day will come. I am growing stronger. I pray for your health.

Vulso read from a second tablet.

Fabia to her beloved Anaximander, many greetings:

Before all else I pray for your health, and daily make supplication on your behalf before the Lord Serapis and the other gods who share his temple. I want you to know that I am alone. Think to yourself: 'My queen is in Rome.' Ever since I left you I have been in mourning, weeping by night and lamenting by day. Do not grieve. We will be together again.

I pray for our good fortune.

"That was probably the first one," commented Vulso, "after she left Ephesus and returned to Rome."

"Listen to this one," said Severus.

Fabia to her most sweet Anaximander, very many greetings:

I received your letter which was brought to me by the sailor. Your letter has given me immense anxiety and

intense distress, most acute pain and burning fever, so
that I have no heart to eat or sleep. You must not come
to me, no matter how much we mourn our separation. I
grieve for our lives if you come.

You must wait and be patient, my sweet fisherman. I
will send for you when it is time. Isis has promised that
we will some day be together.

I pray for your health.

Severus read a fourth tablet.

Fabia to her beloved Anaximander, very many greetings:

The time has come. I send for you. Put off everything and come at once to me. I arranged passage for
you on the merchant ship *Asklepios*. When you come,
stay at the hotel 'Athena's Mantle,' by the Ostia gate.
Then send me a tablet. I will come for you. At last my
eyes will see you again.

I pray for your health before the Lord Serapis and the
Lady Isis. I pray for a safe journey before the Lord and
the Lady.

"That's obviously the most recent," Severus
remarked. "Read the fifth one, Vulso."

Fabia to Anaximander, greetings:

How the gods tamper with us. He was almost dead.
We were almost together. We must wait a little longer,
my beloved. It can't be long now.

I pray for your health.

Vulso tossed the tablet on the table with a flip of his
wrist.

"I don't get it," he said. "Why didn't she just divorce Ferox. It's a relatively simple matter. No court proceedings are necessary."

"She's afraid of him. Or at least she was. What we know of him, his character, is already enough cause for alarm. She knows him better than we."

"Or at least she thought she did when she sent for Anaximander. She may have been wrong."

"Maybe."

"So where are we now?" asked Vulso with a sigh. "We still haven't found Fabia."

"No, but we've made substantial progress. For instance, we now have a good idea of what happened. We can arrange events in their proper sequence." He rose and began to pace the floor. "We know that Anaximander arrived in Rome five days ago, on the eighth day before the Ides. He came because of that letter. Fabia had arranged passage and was expecting him. They would renew their love affair of seventeen years ago. Think of it, Vulso. They waited seventeen years and then they had only one day together."

"How do you know that?"

"Because Anaximander followed instructions. He went to the Athena's Mantle Hotel when he arrived. The next day, the seventh before the Ides, he sent a messenger with the fisherman and queen tablet to Fabia to tell her he was in Rome. She received it, after a week of anxious waiting for the storm delayed ship, and almost immediately left her house with her slave Phryne. She then sent Phryne to the hotel to find Anaximander and bring him to her. That's where our trail ends for the moment."

He sat down on his reading couch. "That was four days ago. We have no information about the next day, the sixth before the Ides. Presumably Fabia and Anaximander spent it together. But the murder of Anaximander took place that night, because the next morning, the morning of the fifth day before the Ides, he was found dead on the steps of the Temple of Mars the Avenger."

"So it's the two days after Anaximander arrived that we have to find out about?"

"Right. Where they were and what happened."

"Do you think she couldn't stand him after all those years and killed him?" asked Vulso tentatively, "or did someone else, Ferox for instance, catch them in bed together and kill them both?"

"The first is not likely. Their reunion must have been a great event for them after seventeen years of waiting. They would be making love and reminiscing. Recapturing the past." He lapsed into thought. "We now have to find Croesus."

"Why Croesus in particular?"

Severus began to tell Vulso about his interview with the praetorian and the visit to the slave market. Halfway through the story, Proculus burst through the door.

"Judge, I'm sorry to disturb you, but it's most important."

"What is it?" said Severus, sitting up.

"It's Straton. He's been badly beaten. A messenger from the *Vigiles*. They found him in the sewer."

"Where is he now? Is he all right?"

"I don't know. He's being attended to by a police doctor. He's at the *Vigiles* station in the Subura. There's a messenger from the *Vigiles* outside."

"We'll go on foot," decided Severus. "It's faster. Proculus, send my litter after me." He headed for the door. "Come on, Vulso."

"Your toga, judge!" yelled Proculus after him. "You're of the Equestrian order. You can't appear in the streets without your toga. It's the law."

Severus pulled his hooded *lacerna* cloak off a hook on the wall in the clerk's office, put it on, and instructed Proculus to put his toga in his closed litter and have it proceed with his lictors as if he were really inside. With that he dashed out the door.

They arrived at the police precinct out of breath. They had practically run the whole way, elbowing and pushing through the dense Subura crowds and sidewalk stalls, weaving in and out side streets, following the messenger and goading him to move faster. Not even the cold rain slowed them down. They were drenched when they arrived at the precinct. Straton was seated on a stool, grinning and holding a slab of veal under his right eye.

"It's to check the swelling," he said when he saw Severus and Vulso stop in the doorway and stare at him.

The doctor was packing his instrument case. "I sponged it with vinegar," he explained matter of factly. "A nasty wound on his left cheek."

"It burned like fire," interjected Straton.

"...I took three stitches," continued the doctor, "and applied a zinc ointment dressing. He's all right, but he'll be a little stiff for a few days. He's bruised all over and may have some broken ribs. I bandaged his torso and tied it with the Hercules knot for luck."

The doctor then left the room. Vulso walked in front of Straton, inspecting his face. "It's lucky that he doesn't make you wear a bandage of hyena skins," he said, "like they do for dog bites."

"I wasn't bitten by a dog. I was trampled by a bull."

"In the Subura district?" asked Severus incredulously.

"Let me tell you what happened."

TWO DAYS BEFORE THE IDES

XIV

VULSO TEACHES TAURUS A HISTORY LESSON

Because the attack on Straton demanded a quick response, Judge Severus put off his visit to Ferox' villa for another day. Instead he met with Vulso and Proculus in his chambers and planned how to deal with the gladiator.

"The transcript of Taurus' previous trial has just arrived from the Tabularium archives," said Proculus, handing the judge a court file, "and your new law assessor Flaccus sent a message saying he was working on the assignment you gave him and would report later this morning."

Severus broke the seal on the file and began to skim through the documents.

"What was Taurus arrested for?" asked Vulso.

"He was tried under the Julian Law on extortion. He was acquitted. From the judge's extract it looks like the witnesses against him either disappeared or changed their stories." He looked up at Vulso from his couch. "How many men are you taking with you?"

"Two *contubernia* of the Urban Cohort — 16 men."

"Be careful. A gladiator, even a has-been, is still dangerous."

"Don't worry, judge. I plan to take him by surprise."

Severus put aside Taurus' file and began scanning through his judge's handbook for guidance with a legal problem, quickly unrolling the scroll to glance at various sections he thought might be pertinent. Finding no answer, he addressed his clerk.

"Quintus, when my new law assessor arrives, have him go to the library and research a problem for me. I want to know whether it is relevant that a defendant, charged with assaulting an officer of the law, did not know who his victim was. Do you understand?"

"Yes. You want to find out whether you can get Taurus for assaulting a law officer or just for assault because he didn't know who Straton really was."

"Exactly. I generally have arbitrary powers in such cases, but I want to ascertain if there's any specific law on it."

"I don't think there is," suggested Proculus, "but I'll tell Flaccus. I assume you want an answer quickly?"

"Right. I don't think Vulso intends wasting any time in bringing Taurus in. Tell Flaccus not to waste any either."

Vulso instructed his troops to loiter about the street outside the tavern and wait, while he and two other uniformed men strode aggressively into Taurus' place.

Vulso grabbed the first slave-waiter he saw. "Court of the Urban Prefect. I want to speak to Taurus."

The slave stared at Vulso and his companions and walked to the stairs at the back of the hall, quickly climbing to the second floor. Vulso and the two soldiers took seats at a table. The taverna was crowded as usual. The customers were too engrossed in their drinking and gambling to pay any attention to a centurion and two soldiers, a common enough sight in any tavern.

The slave returned and told Vulso, "Taurus says you can come upstairs."

"Tell Taurus to come down here."

The slave repeated his hurried trip to the second floor while Vulso took the opportunity to watch the Spanish dancing girls performing the *cordax*. They were licentious enough so that Vulso didn't notice Taurus until he had already taken a seat and asked what he could do for the centurion.

"First bring me and my men *calda*," began Vulso. Taurus called a waiter and placed the order. The drinks were quickly brought.

Vulso took a sip. "I'm looking for a Greek philosopher, name of Straton. He was in the Subura yesterday and may have come in here."

"We don't get many philosophers here," replied Taurus, waving his hand at the crowd.

"You haven't seen him then?"

"Not me. He called a slave-waiter to the table. "Did you see any Greek philosophers here yesterday?"

"No, *domine*."

"You see," said Taurus. "We get mostly fans of the arena here, centurion. What do you want him for anyway?"

"I really didn't think he would come here," said Vulso sidestepping the question. "I only wanted a drink to refresh me and my men — and to meet you. I saw you fight, you know."

"You did?" said the gladiator, relaxing. "Which fight? I had more than 30."

"I don't remember who it was you fought or whether you won. But I remember enjoying your performance."

"I probably won," said Taurus, pleased. "I drew nine times and lost only three fights, and all three times I put up such a good battle that the crowd let me live."

Vulso stood up as if to go. The two soldiers and Taurus did the same.

"That may not have been so fortunate," said Vulso.

"What did you say, centurion?" asked Taurus, not sure he had heard correctly.

Vulso dropped his cup to the floor, shattering it. Taurus automatically looked down. Vulso kicked him right in the groin with his hobnailed boot and smashed him in the head with his swagger stick.

Taurus went down with a gasp. The two soldiers and Vulso drew their swords, giving the signal to the troops outside. They charged into the tavern, while the customers began to scream and scatter.

"Move and you're dead," said Vulso to Taurus who was writhing on the floor clutching his groin. Then, addressing the people in the tavern: "No one leaves. Everyone line up against the walls." He gave an order to his troops. "Search the place. Tear the second floor apart. Bring everyone upstairs down here."

"What's this all about?" croaked Taurus, as the soldiers fanned out and up the stairs.

"Straton, the man you assaulted yesterday, is an officer of the Court of the Urban Prefect and you are under arrest."

"I didn't know who he was," protested Taurus, trying to get up.

Vulso pushed him down with his boot.

"I won't quibble with you and neither will the judge. He said he'll reduce you to the status of a slave, torture you for the information he wants, confiscate your property, brand the name of your crime on your forehead and send you to a forced labor camp."

Taurus got the point. "What information?" he asked sullenly.

Vulso smiled at him. "The judge said to inform you that if you tell me right now where Timotheus lives, and everything you know about him, he will take it into consideration in passing sentence. He has arbitrary powers in such matters, you know. Maybe you can get off lightly, though he's not promising anything. But if you don't cooperate, I can tell you right now that you're done for."

"I want to think it over," mumbled Taurus.

Vulso smiled broadly and called for a piece of chalk. "Do you know the story of Popilius and Antiochus," he asked, while the chalk was being brought to him.

"The story of who?"

"In the time of the Republic," said Vulso, "Antiochus, the Seleucid King of Syria, was at the gates of Alexandria, intending to conquer Egypt. The Roman Senate, however, had decreed that Antiochus should withdraw from Egypt and sent an ambassador, Popilius, with the decree." A soldier handed Vulso a piece of red chalk.

"Well, there was King Antiochus with his whole army, when Popilius strode out of Alexandria alone, armed only with a stick and the decree of the Roman Senate. He gave the king the decree and told him and his army to get out of Egypt. The king replied that he would think it over. Popilius then took his stick and drew a circle in the sand around the king and told him, 'Think it over here'."

Vulso bent down and drew a circle on the floor around Taurus. "Think it over here," he said.

XV

FLACCUS INVESTIGATES
AN OLD DEATH

Flaccus was very pleased with himself. He had carried out his first job as the judge's assessor with speed and success. He peeked out of the curtain of his swaying litter to make sure the litter he was escorting to Judge Severus' chambers was still in front of him. It was, and the two litters had just passed by the Flavian Amphitheater, halfway to the judge's chambers in the Forum of Augustus.

Reassured he flopped back on the pillows and savored in his mind the events of the morning. If the truth be told, he admitted to himself, it was luck rather than his skill that brought success. Still, he was pleased by his luck.

At the archives of the Daily Acts, helped by a competent clerk, he quickly found the obituary of Fabia's deceased lover, Publius Planta. Planta, who was related to a senatorial family, had been a respected lawyer in the City for many years. His body had been discovered at the eighth night hour by a patrol of the *Vigiles* beneath the balcony of his apartment on the Caelian Hill. The Daily Acts, true to its style, gave all the gory details. Planta had landed on his head, cracking it open like an egg. The place where it happened was near the Arch of Drusus and Flaccus hired a litter to take him there. Neighborhood house porters directed him to the right apartment house, where he was informed that Planta's daughter Plotina was still living.

"She's a widow," the porter confided, "and she's always at home."

Plotina wasn't old and she wasn't bad looking, but she gave the impression of being both. Her face was hard set, her body rigid, and her manner precise and formal. Flaccus thought she would probably sit bolt upright, even in a closed litter. Preparing his report to Judge Severus, he reconstructed his conversation with the woman, word for word.

"You want to speak to me about my father?" she asked after her slave showed him into the *tablinum*. She handed back Flaccus' identification with the court's seal and motioned him to a chair across from her.

"Yes, *domina*. Judge Severus, whose assessor I am, is presently investigating a case in which your father's name has cropped up. The case concerns a woman who your father once knew quite well."

Plotina sat stiffly in her chair. "I will of course cooperate with the authorities. What is her name?"

"Her name is Fabia. She's the wife of..."

"I know her. Why, what has happened?"

"She's disappeared. We're trying to trace her."

"I hope it's nothing serious," she said politely, and unconvincingly.

"I'm afraid it is. That's why Judge Severus is asking your help. He's interested in Fabia's background and has been told that Fabia knew your father quite well for a number of years."

"That's correct. I didn't approve of it and told my father so many times. But he was infatuated with her. You see my mother died in childbirth and my father never remarried. But Fabia ensnared him like Circe. My father wanted her to divorce Senator Ferox and marry him."

"Why didn't she?"

Plotina lowered her eyes to the floor. "She was afraid her husband would kill her. I know, because my father often sought my advice. He regarded me as sensible. Unfortunately, the advice he received from me he rarely took. He wanted Fabia. He offered her protection. But Fabia was terrified, or at least that's what she always told my father. I advised him to stop seeing her."

"May I ask why you were opposed to her?"

"I thought she was using my father and didn't really love him. Of course, as his daughter I realize I was prejudiced against her. But that wasn't it. I was opposed because I thought she was not a good woman."

"What makes you say that?"

Plotina shook her head slowly. Her eyes had a far away look. She was remembering, trying to articulate it to herself. Flaccus waited patiently.

"The way she treated my father, for one thing. She treated him the way she treated her slaves. She would humiliate him in public. She would make mean jokes

about him, make fun of him in a cruel way. I don't
know why he stood for it. I once saw her make a slave
grovel in public before she would grant him a favor that
was important to him, but trivial to her. She couldn't
go quite so far with my father, of course, but that was
the idea. It is an unpleasant characteristic and I always
detested her for it. Anyone would, unless like my father
they were blinded by Eros." She paused as if trying to
decide something. A struggle was barely visible on her
face. Then she relaxed. "I also know that she is not a
good woman because she tried to make my father kill her
husband for her."

"What do you mean?" asked Flaccus with surprise.

Her voice was like ice. "Just what I said, assessor.
In the months before my father's death she badgered him
about it constantly. At first he thought she wasn't serious, but later, when he realized she was, I think it opened
his eyes about her. He was in love with her, but he was
not a murderer. If he hadn't died, I think he would have
broken off with her. In fact, assessor, it is my opinion
that he did."

Flaccus looked at her. Her anger was rising. She
was losing control. Her eyes went wild. The words tum-
bled out.

"I have no evidence and I don't want to wrongly
accuse anyone, but it has always been my belief that he
told her he would never see her again and she pushed
him off the balcony." She mustered a weak smile. "But
since there were no witnesses — I was away and he had
sent all the slaves out that night — the *Vigiles* called it an
accident. Still, I am entitled to my opinion."

"I see," said Flaccus. He thought for a moment. "Just for the record, could you tell me where you were on the sixth and seventh days before the Ides? Today is the second."

She looked at him as a mother looks at an innocent child.

"I am not involved with her disappearance. I am a sensible person. But for your record, I am almost always at home and the seventh and sixth were no exception. My slaves were also present."

"Would you come with me to the Forum of Augustus and tell Judge Severus exactly what you have told me?"

"I would appreciate the opportunity, assessor." She stood up. "I will be most happy to go right now."

XVI

VULSO MAKES AN ARREST

Like King Antiochus, it didn't take the gladiator Taurus long to cave in to the demands of Roman authority. He knew that Vulso's threats about enslavement and forced labor camps were not idle talk. His cooperation made it a good bet that he would remain where he was, the proprietor of the taverna, the only difference being that in the future he would have to be an occasional police informer. However, whether he had told the truth about his relationship with Timotheus was still uncertain. Taurus had depicted himself as no more than a local neighborhood strong-arm man, a petty underworld boss, who did "favors" for local residents in return for money. What that meant to Vulso was that Taurus and his gang terrorized those who he was paid to terrorize, extorting money or compliance from them. Timotheus, Taurus had alleged, sometimes wanted such favors done. Discouraging Straton was one of those favors.

Vulso found Timotheus' apartment house just where Taurus said it was. The porter who sat by the entrance of the tenement directed him to the fourth floor. Vulso held his nose as he passed the vat under the staircase in which the feces of the residents were collected, awaiting pickup for later use as fertilizer. He climbed the stairs, found the door to Timotheus' apartment and knocked.

A man opened the door. "I didn't...who are you?" he exclaimed when he saw the centurion. Vulso edged past him into the apartment. It was a typical flat, one small room which served as both living room and sleeping quarters and an even smaller anteroom for a kitchen.

"We're going to have a little Socratic dialogue, Timotheus," said Vulso. "Just you and me. I'll be Socrates and ask the questions. You can give me the answers."

"I'm not answering anything. And I'm not Timotheus. Timotheus isn't here."

"Then who are you? And where is Timotheus?"

"None of your business."

Vulso grabbed him by the tunic with both hands. "You'll speak up before I'm finished with you."

"You can't do that! I'm a free man. A Roman citizen."

Vulso let go and eyed him suspiciously. "If you're a citizen you'll have no objection to answering my questions. I'm an officer of the Court of the Urban Prefect."

"I am a citizen and I do object. Now get out."

Vulso didn't move. "If you're a citizen you can prove it in court, which is where I'm taking you. I'll let the judge ask you what I want to know."

"I'm not going anywhere. I didn't do anything."

"Yes you did. I'm taking you in under the *stellionatus* statute for 'acting like a lizard.' You refuse to give me your name and tell me where Timotheus is. In my opinion that's acting like a lizard. Let's go."

The man didn't reply. He knew it was no use. He walked sullenly down the stairs in front of Vulso. As they reached the street, a procession of priests and priestesses noisily approached from the left. The retinue was singing and dancing wildly, throwing their arms about, pounding blunted swords on metal shields, banging drums, clicking castanets, shaking rattles and blowing trumpets. The priests, smooth-faced eunuchs painted like women, were dressed in armor and hurled themselves into the air and against one another, clanging their armor. The priestesses whirled around, hair tossing, their sounds unintelligible and orgiastic. Celebrants of the Asiatic goddess, Cybele, the Great Mother, they were on the way to their temple, working themselves up for a religious sex orgy. The procession drew the attention of everyone on the street. Vulso casually eyed the priestesses and laughed at the obscene jibes and jokes hurled by hecklers and street loungers watching the parade.

His prisoner, taking advantage of the distraction, suddenly bolted through the procession. Vulso cursed and tore after him, weaving through the crowd, trying to avoid crashing into bystanders. The man turned a corner and dashed up stairs leading to a street on a higher level. Gaining ground, Vulso caught him on the top stair and hauled him down, half tearing the tunic off his back.

"Not so anxious to go to court, are you?" he panted, dragging him to his feet. The centurion twisted his arms behind his back and slammed handcuffs on him. It was then that he noticed the man's back, exposed between the tear of the tunic.

"Citizen's don't often have whipping scars," snorted Vulso. "You're a slave. And probably a runaway at that."

"I'm not a runaway slave," protested the man. "I was a slave. Now I'm free and a citizen. Let me go."

"You can prove it in court," said the centurion, giving him a shove.

The prisoner stood before the tribunal, meeting Judge Severus with the same sullen silence he had maintained since being arrested. On the way in, near forum entrances, he and Vulso had passed several lawyer stations where the advocates loudly advertised their skills and solicited the business of the handcuffed man being dragged by. The prisoner had not responded; not even when the lawyers chased him down the streets, promising success and lowering their fees; not even to their last ditch shouts of "pay me only if you win."

"How can you prove you're a free citizen if you won't tell me your name?" asked Severus in exasperation. "Say who you are and we can confirm your status. If you're a manumitted slave, now free, the records will be with the praetor."

The man remained silent, just glaring at Severus and his aides seated around him.

"If you won't say who you are, at least tell me where Timotheus is and how you came to be in his apartment."

The man bent his head and looked at the floor.

But Severus had a hunch about his identity. He turned to his assessor Flaccus and briefly discussed the applicability of a legal precedent for what he had in mind. They nodded their heads in agreement and the judge turned back to face the prisoner.

"Take your clothes off!" he ordered.

The man didn't move. Severus nodded to his two court lictors, one of whom held him by the shoulders while the other pulled off his tunic.

Everyone — Severus, Vulso, Proculus, Flaccus, the court attendants – stared at the nude man. Vulso laughed out loud. Severus couldn't resist a comment.

"You *are* richly endowed, Croesus," he said, grinning.

Croesus looked shocked. "How do you...?" The question remained stuck in his mouth.

Severus' voice turned cold. "It hardly matters. I know who you are. I've been looking for you. And I want some answers."

"I won't answer anything," Croesus replied defiantly.

"You'll answer my questions now or you'll answer under torture. First I want to know where Timotheus is, then how you came to be in his apartment, and then I want to know where Fabia is."

Croesus made no response.

"Do you want time to think it over?" asked Severus nicely.

No reply.

"Answer or be tortured," Severus threatened.

Croesus glared at him.

"One last chance, you fool."

Croesus didn't reply.

"Proculus," said the judge, keeping his eyes fastened on Croesus, "make out the court order for the judicial torture of the slave, Croesus. Arrange it for tomorrow morning."

XVII

THE SLAVES OF FEROX AND
FABIA HOLD A MEETING

The slaves of the household of Ferox and Fabia came singly and in small groups into the peristyle of the mansion. They gathered on one side of the fish pond, the first to arrive taking seats on the marble benches, others leaning against statues, columns or the frescoed walls. Worried and tense, they spoke in hushed voices. "Why has Menelaus called us together?" asked a new arrival. "I don't know," answered another. "I heard that he received a message-tablet from Judge Severus a few minutes ago," offered a third. "What does he want from us now? We were in court the day before yesterday," complained the first, a look of helplessness in his eyes. "Maybe he wants to question us again," said another. "He's going to have us tortured," trembled a young woman slave. "Don't panic," said another, rushing to comfort her. But it was on all their minds.

To the law a slave was a *res* – a thing; to society, often more realistic than the law, a slave was at least an animal; to philosophers, often more realistic than society, a slave was a fellow human fallen upon misfortune. But while philosophers would console slaves with the insight that their souls, if not their bodies, were free, and while many good and compassionate people in society treated their slaves as members of the family, the law was relentless in its abstraction. Thus news of a message from a Roman judge was sure to be viewed with trepidation: slaves rarely feared philosophers; often they feared their masters; but they always feared the law.

Harpax, Probus and Tisander, chiefs of *decuriae*, the squads of ten into which the household slaves were divided, and next in charge after Menelaus, entered together, their faces grim. Harpax was Fabia's slave. He was manager of the storerooms, but for all his access to food, he was skin and bones and looked unhealthy and worn out. One of his eyes twitched constantly in nervousness. It was he who had fetched the sprig of cypress and hung it on the door of Ferox' sick room.

Probus belonged to Ferox. He had been bought because his full voice and precise diction recommended him as the senator's reader. After a while, Ferox had appointed him *silentarius*, enforcer of silence among the slaves in the house, as well as copyist, librarian, secretary and keeper of the household pets. With the combined disappearance of Fabia and the absence of Ferox, Probus encouraged volubility and for the past few days had gone around the house stirring up conversations. Tisander was *procurator*, in charge of purchasing and outside business. He was clever and somewhat sneaky. In the absence of the senator and his wife, Tisander had discarded the rough garments which Ferox had decreed for his slaves and instead came to the meeting dressed in one of the senator's best tunics.

Of the twenty-seven other slaves present in the house, there were fifteen females and twelve males; a mixture of ages and nationalities. None had been born into the *familia*, though most had been born into slavery. There were kitchen slaves and cleaning slaves, messenger slaves and shopping slaves. There were litter-bearers chosen for their physical strength and clerks for their proficiency with numbers. There was a walking-stick slave selected for his short, stocky build, whose job it was to accompany his master and serve as a leaning post when Ferox was standing. And there was a *nomenclator*, whose task it was to remember the names of all the people his master had met and remind him in time. There were masseurs, keepers of the wardrobes, a gardener, a musician and entertainers and an astrologer.

Menelaus walked to the center of the group, held up a message-tablet and called for silence. "This is the reason I asked us to come together. It's from Judge Severus. He says he has captured Croesus in Timotheus' apartment and that further information about Fabia, Ferox and Anaximander compels him to interview us again. He will be here within a few hours." A growing murmur and a few protests were hushed by the chief slave. "We have to decide what to do. We don't want trouble from him. We want to end the investigation quickly but we have to protect ourselves. If we don't, no one will. Above all, we have to avoid giving him a reason to have us tortured."

"We've already told him enough," interrupted the walking-stick slave. "What more does he want? I don't like this."

"Why does he want to question us again?" said one of the litter-bearers. "Why doesn't he question Ferox? Is he trying to pin this on us?"

"We shouldn't tell him anything more," suggested a cooking slave. "Let's keep quiet now."

"What!" shot back Tisander, "and have him think we're not cooperating. He'd be sure to torture us then. We have to tell him something. I don't care what it is – we can decide – but we can't be silent."

"Then this is an opportunity," joined in Probus in his mellifluous voice. "Why don't we now tell him we think Ferox killed Fabia and Anaximander?"

"And get ourselves into more trouble?" countered Harpax. "How can we tell a Roman judge that a Roman senator is a murderer? Slaves can't make accusations like that against patricians. The judge will make us pay, out of spite if nothing else. The upper classes stick together, remember, especially against slaves."

"The judge didn't seem a bad sort in the courtroom," answered Probus. "Maybe we can make the accusation in confidence."

"You're crazy," interjected the astrologer. "He's a Roman judge. We're slaves. That's all you have to know. I've had experiences with the law before. Slaves don't get breaks and accusing their master of a crime is asking for real trouble."

They all began shouting at once. Menelaus called them to order. "Please, stop wrangling. We haven't much time and we have to agree on what we're going to tell him."

"I have an idea," suggested Tisander. "Suppose we don't tell him outright that we think Ferox did it, but tell him some more stories about how Ferox hated Fabia. It's the truth, isn't it? Didn't he say he wished her dead many times? I heard him say so..." "So did I," added a kitchen slave. "And I heard it too," chimed in several others at once. "See," continued Tisander, "we can do it that way. Just like we decided before we went to court. That way, if we continue to feed him information voluntarily, he won't torture us for it."

"We should also get him to question Ferox," commented the walking-stick slave. "He'll see for himself that Ferox is insane. Ferox will make himself look guilty."

"Suppose Ferox is lucid when the judge sees him?" asked a clerk-slave. "What then?"

"Don't worry," answered a shopping slave. "When the judge mentions Fabia, as he's sure to do, Ferox won't be lucid for long."

A young boy at the back joined in. "I have a good idea. We already told him all the true stories about Ferox and Fabia. Why don't we make up a few more? No one will know the difference. We can say that Ferox already tried to kill her once before. We didn't tell him in court because we were afraid. We..."

"No!" Menelaus cut him off. "We already agreed to stick to the truth. It's much safer. We might make a slip if we invented a story. Then he would surely have us tortured. I agree with Tisander. Tell him about the death threats. We can say it occurred to us after leaving court. Or we were afraid then or didn't realize its importance. And I agree we should get him to see Ferox as soon as possible. After he's seen him, he'll have more proof — and from Ferox himself. That's the best way. Stay with what we've already decided." He looked around for comments. No one disagreed. "All right. Then that's decided. Now what about Croesus and Timotheus. He'll want to know what we know about them. What do we say?"

"What is there to say?" asked a litter-bearer. "They're thick as thieves. They were when Croesus was still here."

"The judge will want to know," said Tisander, "whether we knew Croesus was in Rome."

The slaves looked at each other to see if anyone had a good answer.

"We can safely say we didn't know," suggested Harpax after a few moments indecision. "He hasn't been around here in the past year, has he? So how are we supposed to know where he was? If we tell him we knew, he'll only want to know why we didn't tell him before. It'll only get us into trouble."

"He'll also want to know whether we think Croesus or Timotheus had anything to do with the disappearance of Fabia," continued Tisander.

"How does he expect us to know?" replied Menelaus. "All we can tell him is that at least while Croesus lived here he hated Fabia for her humiliating treatment and Ferox for his brutality. Anyway, we've decided Ferox caused her disappearance, so if we're asked, we hint at that. As for Timotheus, we all know what a parasite he is, how he always took Ferox' side and encouraged him to treat us harshly. Anything bad anyone wants to say about Timotheus is all right. Just make sure the judge knows that Timotheus does Ferox' bidding."

There was a knock at the door. One slave went to answer it, while the rest hurriedly dispersed. "Relax," called the slave from the door, "it's only Metronax from the villa."

Everyone streamed back into the peristyle. Metronax handed Menelaus a message-tablet. He read it and smiled broadly. "Metronax has brought us a copy of a message that Judge Severus sent to Ferox today," he announced. "It says that the judge will travel to the villa to question Ferox tomorrow."

Everyone cheered.

.

XVIII

MARCUS FLAVIUS SEVERUS :
TO HIMSELF

Sometimes, when I am hearing a case, as I sit there on the tribunal, I say to myself I am not Marcus Flavius Severus. I wipe my mind of my identity and fill it instead with the persona of a Plato or a Zeno or an Epicurus or Seneca, as if one of them were judging. My ideal, presumptuous though it may be, is to decide like a philosopher-king – Plato's ideal. But I know I can only give an approximation, for even though I am intimately familiar with the writings of these men, I do not really know, in the deepest sense, what kind of men they were. I can only think what type of men I would esteem them to be. Why is this? Because how can we really know others; we barely know ourselves. The more deeply I delve into a case, the more I peel away the levels of the human mind, like peeling off the skins of an onion one at a time. Human actions seem to me almost like the moves in a game of *latrunculi*, where behind each move there is an enormous complexity of possibilities, thoughts and variations, never expressed, never brought to light, but which nevertheless are the real backdrop to what is actually played out. Is the game the moves that are actually played? Or is it those which are thought of, whether played or not?

Today I ordered a slave to be tortured. That was the move I played. The variations which went through my mind, which are still going through it, are another matter. Does a philosopher-king act this way too? Is his mind a turmoil of possibilities and variations? How can he calmly see his way to a direct result? And that is not the only problem that disturbs me. There is another, perhaps a more important one. Even assuming I can act like a philosopher-king, what guarantee, indeed what hint, do I have that anything worthwhile can be accomplished. Even Plato failed as a philosopher-king in Syracuse. My eyes are not closed to the corruption of our society. And not ours alone. The Greeks, before we pacified them, fought incessant, pointless wars; the Egyptians worship monsters; the Persians are slaves to one man; the barbarians are barbarians. It is an open secret that our soon-to-be emperor, Marcus Aurelius, hates the gladiatorial games. But can he do anything about them? Of the two, he is the more expendable. The populace would prefer the games to the philosopher-king. That is the way it is, with variations, in all nations. So what hope have I, who must follow the constraints of our laws and customs, of ever conforming my conduct to the Law of Nature which Alexander often urges upon me, and which I strive to attain? Therefore, I follow the standard practice in dealing with a slave who withholds information about a murder. I order him tortured. Would Zeno do it? Would Plato or Seneca? Would a philosopher-king? Perhaps. Perhaps not.

ONE DAY BEFORE THE IDES

XIX

A JUDICIAL TORTURE AND A
HORRIBLE DISCOVERY

"Have you ever seen a slave-witness questioned under judicial torture?" asked Severus while he and his assessor Flaccus were on their way to conduct the examination of Croesus.

"I've seen the *carnifex* torture slaves and carry out public executions in the Esquiline field, and I've seen criminals tortured and executed in the arena, but I'm not sure whether some public torture I've seen was judicial or not. I have studied the applicable law, however."

"Then you are familiar with the legal protections and safeguards under Roman law?"

"Yes, judge. I was taught that because witnesses often lie to escape the pain, the Imperial Constitutions state that 'confidence should not always be placed in torture,' although, of course, 'it ought not to be rejected as entirely untrustworthy.' Indeed, if I remember correctly, the law says that it is usually not until after a case has been fully investigated that it can be decided whether confidence is to be placed in torture or not."

"Even more important," interjected Severus pedagogically, "are the rescripts which embody specific protections. A rescript of Trajan holds 'the magistrate should not ask the witness being tortured whether he committed the crime, but rather he should ask in general terms who did it, for a leading question seems to suggest an answer rather than to ask for one.' In addition, a recent rescript of our emperor says that someone who has made a confession implicating himself shall not be tortured to obtain evidence against others. It is also the rule that a confession alone is insufficient to prove the crime; there must be other evidence to corroborate it."

They entered a small room where the inquiry was to take place. "I have ordered," explained the judge, "this torture to be held in secret rather than — as is usual — in public. Public torture is a exemplary warning of judicial power and a demonstration that the State is doing all it can to solve a crime, but I don't want knowledge of what we find out to circulate just yet."

Two soldiers of the Urban Cohort were strapping a naked Croesus to a 'Y' shaped pole, the *furca*. His head was pushed into the opening of the two 'V' shaped beams, to which his arms were fastened. The *quaestionarius*, wearing a red cap to signify his dreaded calling, tested the feel of his whip which was loaded with lead balls interspersed among the thongs. Proculus, the court clerk, sat on a stool ready to take down the interrogation for the judicial record.

Severus took his place on the magistrate's chair that Proculus had set up for him, along with the statue of Jupiter Fidius, the god of Good Faith, whose presence turned the chamber into an official courtroom. Flaccus sat on Severus' right and assumed a judicial air. The judge's lictors stood at attention on either side of him. He addressed Croesus.

"I'll give you one last chance to avoid this. Just answer my questions."

Croesus spat at Severus, who then nodded to the *quaestionarius*. He stepped behind the slave and hit him with a vicious blow on his back. Proculus looked away. Flaccus gasped. Severus flinched. Globules of blood immediately welled up. Croesus groaned.

"What is your name?" asked Severus. "Who owns you?"

Croesus spat again.

"Come on," said the judge. "I already know the answers to those questions. There is no purpose in taking a beating over such information."

Croesus didn't answer. Severus nodded at the *quaestionarius* who applied the whip. Croesus grunted in pain. He still didn't answer. The torturer hit him again. This time Croesus screamed and his back turned red with blood.

"My name is Croesus," he gasped. "I am a slave of Fabia, wife of Lucius Junius Ferox."

"Where do you live?"

Croesus shut his eyes and clenched his teeth in anticipation of the blow.

"It's only a question for the record," rejoined Severus. "Just tell me where you live."

Croesus didn't answer. The whip whistled through the air and thudded into his back. Croesus screamed in agony.

"In an apartment," he said "by the wooden statue."

"Where is that?"

"Behind the statue of Vertumnus the Etruscan, on the Vicus Tuscus, the third floor."

"Tell me what you know about the murder of Anaximander and the disappearance of Fabia."

Croesus opened his eyes wide in amazement. The *quaestionarius* gave him another terrific blow. Croesus made a long agonized scream and passed out. A soldier pushed a sponge soaked with vinegar into the slave's face. He opened his eyes.

"Tell me what you know about the murder of Anaximander and the disappearance of Fabia," repeated Severus.

Croesus didn't answer. He hardly screamed at the blow which followed, then lost consciousness. The soldier again applied the vinegar. Croesus barely reacted and groaned continuously.

"We'll have to try tomorrow, *eminentissime*," suggested the *quaestionarius*. "He has no endurance. Any more today would be like trying to get water from pumice, as they say."

"We'll need another court order then," said Proculus, turning to Severus. "Shall I prepare it?"

Severus rose from his chair sullenly and headed toward the door. Flaccus and Proculus followed quickly in his wake. They walked back to the judge's chambers in silence. Vulso and Straton, who had been waiting, asked what they had found out.

"Nothing," said Flaccus. "The slave refused to talk."

Severus stood at the door. "Come with me," he said to his aides. "Proculus, have you sent a messenger to Ferox telling him that I'm coming to see him this morning?"

"Yes, judge."

"Now send another messenger to say that I've been detained and won't be able to see him until this afternoon."

"Where are we going," asked Vulso, "if not to see Ferox?"

"He'll have to wait. We have a more urgent trip to make right now. And eggs today are better than chickens tomorrow."

"More important than Ferox?" wondered Straton, a little confused.

"Yes. Croesus gave me an important piece of information. He told me where he lived."

"What's so important about that?" asked Vulso.

"If my deduction is right," replied the judge, "Anaximander was murdered in Croesus' apartment."

Severus and Vulso climbed the steps of the apartment house behind the wooden statue of Vertumnus, two at a time. Straton, still hindered by his injuries, ascended more slowly. Vulso tried the door. "It's locked," he said.

"Everybody in Rome locks their doors. Break it down."

Vulso crashed into it twice before it gave way. The three men stood at the threshold and gazed inside. The two room apartment looked like the arena. Dried blood was spattered on the floor and walls. Every piece of furniture was overturned – table, double bed, chest, cooking grill. The shutters were closed. Shards from smashed

oil lamps and food jars were scattered all over. The floor
was sticky with a mixture of spilled wine and blood.
Small pottery statues of what may once have been the
gods Isis and Serapis were in fragments.

Severus walked about the rooms, picking up pieces
of broken objects. "It looks like there was a wild fight,"
he said. "They must have fought for their lives." He
turned the chest right side up. "Books and clothes," he
commented, examining the contents. "Love poems of
Catullus; one in Greek, the Idylls of Theocritus; a book
of erotic Alexandrian epigrams by Asclepiades." He
tossed the books back into the chest and began pulling
out clothes. "Expensive stuff," he remarked. "Silk from
China, tunics of Miletian wool." He held up a flimsy
garment. "Look at this one, Vulso. You can see through
it, it's so fine."

Straton walked to the window and opened the shutters. "It smells horribly in here," he complained.

"Spilled perfume," said Severus. "Olive oil base
turned rancid." He noticed a lead vessel on its side and
put it to his nose. "Oil of roses." He spotted another
vessel, sniffed it, picked up a lead vial and read the label
which dangled from it. "Panther scent, from Tarsus."
Vulso found a fourth leaden jar. "Oil of saffron from
Rhodes, it says." The threw it back on the floor.

"There are more perfume vials in the chest, along
with different unguents," said Severus. He inspected
the kitchen room. It was well stocked with bread, flour,
spices, fruits, vegetables, meats, wine, water.

"No wonder Croesus refused to talk," said Vulso.
"But it doesn't matter now, we have the evidence to con-
vict him."

"What evidence?" said Severus.

"Well, he lived here, didn't he. It's his apartment and all this stuff obviously belonged to Fabia. She was killed here, along with Anaximander and Phryne. Who knew they were here except for Croesus?"

"Don't jump to conclusions. Maybe Croesus was involved in the murder, maybe not. We can't be sure. But it does look, from the amount of the damage, like there might have been more than one assailant and more than one victim. So even if Croesus were involved, he might not have been the only one. And if he were involved, was he the instigator or was he someone else's tool?"

"He could have told Timotheus that Fabia would be here," suggested Straton. "He was staying in Timotheus' apartment, after all. And Timotheus could have hired that gladiator Taurus. Only a butcher like Taurus could have done all this."

Severus hadn't heard Straton. He stood between the two rooms, turning his head from the one to the other, examining first the living room and then the kitchen, then back to the living room.

"You know," he said finally, "I thought before we came here that this was the murder scene. My theory must be basically correct. But it's just hard to believe the logic of it."

"What is on your mind?" asked Vulso.

Severus didn't appear to hear him either. "Even if I accept the logic of it," he went on, "I still don't understand the implications. Ferox and Timotheus. It's now time to talk to Ferox and Timotheus."

XX

SEVERUS VISITS FEROX
AT HIS VILLA

The trip from the Flaminian Gate to Ferox' villa took three hours. Severus and Vulso rode in a four-horse covered carriage, whiling away the time playing *latrunculi*. They moved the black and white *calculi* rapidly, in the confident manner of experienced players, though there were occasional long thoughts over a move. With a sudden combination the judge forced the centurion to resign the game. The two players briefly analyzed the moves and discussed improvements for each side. Then they switched colors.

"How did you know the murder took place in Croesus' apartment?" asked Vulso, arranging his pieces for the second game.

"The other day in my chambers I wondered about Fabia and Anaximander's first meeting after seventeen years. I thought Fabia would have treated it as an event and staged it to recapture the past. So I reconstructed it in my mind and that led me to Croesus' apartment."

"What was the connection?"

"Fabia's slave, Menelaus, if you'll remember, told us that in Ephesus they carried on the affair in Anaximander's flat."

"He mentioned it was a small one, near a Temple of Serapis," recalled Vulso.

"Correct. Now when Anaximander arrived in Rome last week, Fabia didn't meet him at the ship and she didn't have him come to her home in the City. She sent Phryne to the Athena's Mantle Hotel and Phryne brought Anaximander to Fabia. Where? An apartment somewhere in the City seemed most likely. What kind of an apartment? Probably a small intimate one for an intimate reunion after seventeen years. One like their love nest in Ephesus would do nicely."

"But there are countless places like that in Rome," countered Vulso. "It could have been anywhere. How did you figure out it was Croesus'?"

"I reasoned that one place it might be was Croesus'. Fabia had bought Croesus back from the slave dealer and must have kept him somewhere in the City. A small flat was most probable. And when you found Croesus staying at Timotheus' apartment in the Subura, it occurred to me that if Croesus is staying at someone else's apartment, it might very well be because someone else was staying at his."

Vulso gave a little laugh and made the first move of the second game. Severus replied quickly. Their minds dove into the game. They were in the midst of a tricky tactical situation when the coachman called down from his perch that the milestone before the turn-off to Ferox' villa had been reached.

Severus told the driver to stop, got out, and signalled to a carriage which had trailed them from the City.

"Straton," he called to the driver of the second vehicle, "this is the milestone before the turn-off. You wait here."

With a wave of his hand Straton turned his carriage around, facing back towards Rome. He drove off the paved road onto the gravel shoulder which paralleled the highway, maneuvered the coach under a shady pine tree, jumped down from his driver's perch and began to loosen one of the wheels. Carefully positioning it so that his vehicle would appear disabled to anyone curious or suspicious about his presence at that spot, he placed the wheel where he could quickly refix it when his mission called for him to move again.

Vulso walked to the middle of the road, checked the time with a small sun dial held in the palm of his hand, and then joined the coachman to help the judge, standing by the side of the road, put on his toga for a proper entrance into Ferox' villa.

"Remember," called Severus to Straton as the garment was being wound around him, "after we leave, you pick up anyone or follow any wagon that leaves Ferox' villa. Court slaves are waiting at the Flaminian Gate to take up the trail from there. You're in charge. Send me a message late tonight or earlier if it's urgent."

"Right, judge. Good luck."

The judge remounted his carriage for the remainder of the trip to Ferox' villa.

Severus and Vulso drove along a path from the main road to the front of the villa. The house looked a bit dilapidated and weathered. Peeling paint testified that it was not in good repair.

Two slaves waited for the vehicle to stop. One held a colorful Persian-style umbrella between Severus and the sun as the judge stepped down from the coach, while the other one bowed in greeting and held the judge's toga hem from touching the ground.

"Welcome, most eminent judge Marcus Flavius Severus," he said. "My master, the most illustrious Lucius Junius Ferox has instructed me to escort you to the garden for refreshments. He will join you there."

Severus and Vulso followed the slave. It was a simple garden, quite below the standards for the country place of a member of the Senatorial class. There was no sleeping pavilion, no riding course, no complicated fountains or expensive statues, no sculpted box-shrubs or exotic trees and plants. Only a few inexpensive marble benches could be seen, the usual local flora, and some statuary, including the customary erect phallus statue of the god Priapus to symbolize and encourage germination and fruitfulness and to ward off evil. Yet despite its meager appointments and a somewhat unkempt appearance, the garden was cool and pleasant.

Two slave boys, both of whom looked effeminate and no older than twelve, brought refreshments. A pet snake slithered through the grass.

Severus and Vulso had hardly taken a sip of cold wine when Ferox entered the garden. He was dressed in a tunic of inexpensive material. His head was bald – perhaps another Stoic affectation, thought Severus – and his face creased with sharply chiseled lines. He wore a fashionable short clipped beard and looked strong and brutal. His mouth curled slightly downward at the edges in a perpetual scowl. He exchanged a polite greeting kiss with Severus.

"You are the judge from the Court of the Urban Prefect?"

"Yes, most illustrious," answered Severus politely. "And this is my aide Caius Vulso."

Ignoring the introduction, Ferox sat down on a bench opposite Severus and Vulso. "And you have come to ask me about the disappearance of my wife."

"How did you know that?" asked Severus.

"Why else would you be here?"

"I meant how did you know your wife disappeared? When did you learn it?"

"When?" said Ferox annoyed. "When it happened. The next day. What's the difference? One of my slaves here went to the town house. Everyone was talking about it. How could I not know? When my slave arrived that old fool Menelaus was even reporting it to the Urban Prefect. I'm surprised it took you so long to come here." He glared at Severus, staring him right in the eye. "Have you found her body yet?"

Severus stared right back at him. "How do you know she's dead?"

"What other explanation could there be? She's not the type to run away without letting everyone know. No one would want to hold her prisoner and there has been no ransom demand. She's not at home. So she must be dead."

"Since you seem so well informed, perhaps you know who killed her?"

"I did," began Ferox. Vulso almost jumped up to arrest him. "My Stoic beliefs make me realize my guilt. I am ultimately responsible for her death."

"But I meant, of course," interrupted Severus, "that you might know or suspect who actually killed her."

"I know that's what you meant, Severus, and the answer is that I resent your coming here and asking me all these questions." His temper flared.

Severus stopped him with a look. "You have no cause to resent the questions, Ferox. I have done you the courtesy of conducting this interview at your villa, rather than subpoenaing you into court in Rome. But this is a murder investigation. I am the *cognitio* judge. I have full authority to question you and I insist on your answering. If not here, then in court. That you are of the Senatorial class will not count in this instance. I invoke the power and authority of Roman law."

Ferox gave Severus a frigid stare. "I don't know who killed her."

"Now," said Severus, "what do you know about Anaximander?"

"Who is Anaximander?" asked Ferox.

"You don't know?"

"Should I?"

"Anaximander," announced Severus, "is the lover your wife had in Ephesus."

"That was almost twenty years ago," replied Ferox.

"That's right. What do you know about him?"

"Only what she told me."

"Did you know of your wife's affair when you were in Ephesus?"

"Not at the time. Later my wife made sure to tell me all about him. She didn't spare any details. She said she loved only him and hated me. She told me that frequently. She tried to taunt me with it." He looked at Severus and smirked. "I fixed her. I told her that it was too bad she loved him so much because if he ever came to Rome or if she ever went back to Ephesus, I would kill them both. She was free, I told her, to have any other affairs she liked." He stared into the distance above Severus' head.

"Why did you make such a distinction?"

"It was only the first betrayal that counted. The rest means nothing." He looked grim. "And I never forget anything. Never." His mind was now far away. "I hated her and she hated me," he intoned. "I thought she would win. She was more powerful in the end. But now I've triumphed. She's dead and I'm alive. It was Divine Providence, just as the Stoics say."

"Couldn't you divorce?"

"Why should we divorce? I needed her money and she needed my status."

"Did you kill her?"

"I deny it."

"Did you know that Anaximander was in Rome?"

"I did not."

"Did you kill Anaximander?"

"I did not."

"But you admit that you tried to destroy Fabia for years. You were trying to kill her subtly, but not directly. Is that right? Do you expect me to believe that?"

"Believe what you like. I state that I was trying to kill my wife in my own way and in my own time. If someone murdered her within the past few days, he has deprived me of my real victory. You see, I wanted to drive her to commit suicide just as she wanted me to kill myself."

Severus and Vulso exchanged a quick glance. They were both thinking the same thing — that Ferox was unbalanced.

"Did Fabia tell you," persevered Severus, "that she had sent for Anaximander? That Anaximander was coming to Rome?"

"No, she didn't tell me. She would have. She was planning something – that's why she sent for him." Ferox spoke as if he were thinking out loud. "He was her final move. She sent for him. She was going to leave me for him. Then I would have to kill him and her or kill myself. One or the other. She was gambling that I would kill myself, that I hadn't the strength any more to kill them. That's why she sent for him." He began to laugh in an uncontrollable fashion. "And someone else killed them," he went on between peals of laughter. "What irony. I think I shall write a play about it." He laughed again. "I must tell Timotheus. He will appreciate the irony." Severus and Vulso just waited him out, exchanging looks.

Severus thought of a famous old case, during the reign of Tiberius, when a senator was accused of throwing his wife out of the window. He feigned innocence and insanity until his guilt was proved. Then he committed suicide. Could Ferox be pretending insanity? Or was he really unbalanced? Could it be a little of both? Severus continued the questioning.

"Do you know that your wife bought the slave Croesus after you sold him?"

"Of course. She told me. She let me know that she had him in an apartment somewhere in the City and that she would visit him often. Do you see how degraded she was. She would even sleep with slaves to humiliate me."

Severus gave him a quizzical look. "What about Phryne? What was your and your wife's relationship to her? Why did you buy her, for instance?"

"I bought her for my pleasure, of course. After Fabia told me of her affairs. I enjoyed Phryne for a long time. But then Fabia seduced her when I was sick and stole her away."

Severus leaned his chin on his hands and stared at Ferox. "Tell me about Timotheus."

"Timotheus is my philosopher. We discuss philosophy and confidences. I get his companionship, support and advice. He lives off me and hopes for a bequest. I shall not disappoint him, by the way." He laughed. "Yes, I made sure to leave Timotheus something to remember me by."

That sounds bad for Timotheus, Vulso thought. Straton will like that.

"Did Timotheus and Fabia get along well?"

"Ask him. He's inside the house."

"I will ask him," said Severus, pleased that Timotheus had been dropped into his lap. "But now I'm asking you."

Ferox made an effort to control his temper at Severus' brusque manner. He succeeded and lapsed into a monotone.

"She tried to steal him from me, alienate him from me, like she did with Croesus and Phryne. But this time it didn't work. Timotheus resisted. He has the strength of his philosophy. That's why I can rely on him. why I know his philosophy is sound. Because it enabled him to resist her. My association with him enabled me to resist her." He sounded unbalanced again. "I almost died two years ago. I was at her mercy then. But Timotheus gave me the strength to carry on. Timotheus and the philosophy of Stoicism."

"For the record. Ferox, when was the last time you were in Rome."

"I haven't been there for more than two weeks. I've been here all the time."

"Has Timotheus also been here with you all that time?"

"No. He spends an occasional day or two in Rome. I don't remember which ones."

"How many slaves do you have here at the villa?"

"Four. I don't need many any more. Not since I've been won over to Stoic simplicity."

"Vulso will want to interview them now." said Severus, nodding at Vulso to go into the house and talk to the slaves. "Meanwhile, Senator Ferox. I will talk to Timotheus and you are to consider yourself under house arrest. Please confine your movements to this villa and its grounds."

XXI

JUDGE SEVERUS TALKS TO TIMOTHEUS

A hot afternoon sun blazed in a cloudless sky when Severus and Vulso took the philosopher Timotheus for a walk in the meadow behind Ferox' villa. They left him under a plane tree and walked to the top of a rise where they could talk without being overheard, yet still observe Timotheus under the tree and Ferox puttering in his garden.

"What do you think, Vulso," asked Severus, "is Ferox crazy or not?"

"His manner is consistent with the stories we've heard about him, but it comes across more strongly in person. My opinion is that Senator Ferox is unbalanced. Capable of anything."

The judge agreed. "He certainly reminds me more of Caligula than Cato." He looked in Ferox' direction. "What did the slaves have to say?"

"Besides those two fawning 'speaking tools' who met us in front of the villa, there's only the two slave-boys.

They run most of the errands and it was one of them who told Ferox about Fabia's disappearance after he heard about it at the house in the City. I assume, sir, that you noticed their appearance."

"I could hardly miss it. I thought at first they were girls, not young boys. But, of course, I'm sure Ferox knows exactly what they are. He bought them, didn't he?"

"Yes. Within the past year."

"Another burst of Stoic enthusiasm, no doubt. What did the slaves have to say about Ferox' movements?"

"They confirm his story that he was here for the past two weeks, although they all admit there were long periods during certain days when he was out of sight, either when one of them was away or when Ferox was taking a walk away from the villa. Also they can't account for Ferox during most of the nights. They assume he was asleep, just as they were. They can't remember anything special about the seventh or sixth days before the Ides."

"So the possibility that Ferox went to Rome to murder his wife is not physically excluded."

"I would say that's correct. He could have done it. There are horses here and wagons he could have driven to Rome without anyone at the villa knowing — or telling."

They walked back to the plane tree where Timotheus was waiting. Severus motioned to him to remain put and he and Vulso sat on the grass, the judge first taking the time to unwind his toga and fold it up neatly. He looked at the philosopher carefully. Timotheus was thin, with deep set eyes and a wary expression.

"Tell me, Timotheus," said Severus in Greek, "is Ferox insane?" Though Timotheus wasn't expecting the question, he launched into a lecture.

"What is, and what is not, a sound mind?" he asked rhetorically, extending an arm in practiced fashion. "If we consider..."

Severus cut him off. "Stop it. I want straight answers from you. Otherwise the centurion will take you over that rise and talk some sense into you, if you understand me."

Timotheus understood. "I'm sorry, *eminentissime*," he apologized, assuming an ingratiating tone. "You can't blame me for trying, can you? It satisfies some people."

"By 'some people' you mean Senator Ferox, don't you?"

"I suppose so," acknowledged Timotheus.

"Is he crazy?"

"Let us say," replied Timotheus carefully, "that he occasionally loses touch with reality."

"How often is occasionally?"

"When I am with him, it is not too bad. We talk about philosophy."

"Why do you, a professed Greek philosopher, spend your time with a near-lunatic?" asked Severus with a touch of scorn edged in his voice.

Timotheus flashed a wry smile. "I'm not one of those endowed professors who hold imperial chairs in philosophy at 100,000 sesterces a year, nor do I have a reputation which would bring rich students flocking to sit at my feet. I don't know who you studied with, *eminentissime*, whether it was Fronto or Favorinus in Rome or Herodes Atticus or Calvisius Taurus in Athens, but I'll wager that when you were considering the various possibilities, you did not consider Timotheus."

Severus had to admit that was true.

"Once," continued Timotheus, "I tried to live in a hut outside a city to gain a reputation, like Proteus Peregrinus did outside of Athens. But no one paid any attention to me. Do you know how difficult it is for philosophers like me? We have to eke out money by scrounging off the rich. 'Shadows' they call us. 'Parasites.' We have to find a patron sometimes just to stay alive. Why are we parasites any more than the rich Romans who keep us around to acquire a veneer of culture? So Ferox is a little crazy. What of it? If Seneca could spend his time teaching Nero, I can spend mine teaching Ferox. I don't harm him and he gets full value from me."

Severus assumed a friendly air. "Now, Timotheus, perhaps you can help me. You heard about Fabia, haven't you? About what happened?"

"I've heard from Ferox that she has disappeared."

"Do you know what might have happened to her?"

"I know exactly what happened to her. I even know where you can find her?"

"Yes?"

"You will find her in an apartment near the Vicus Tuscus. She uses it for her love affairs. She's there now with a lover and has been for about a week."

"How do you know this?"

"The apartment is usually occupied by one of her slaves named Croesus. Croesus and I are friends. We met when he was a slave in Ferox' *familia*. About two weeks ago he came to my Subura flat and asked if he could stay with me for a while. He said Fabia had told him to stock his apartment with provisions and then leave until further notice. I let Croesus stay at my place, particularly since I intended to be with Ferox here at the villa most of the time."

"Why did Fabia tell Croesus to stock the apartment and leave?"

"An affair is my guess."

"Has she done this before? Stayed with a lover? Is that how you know?"

"Not exactly. But what other reason could there be. I know that Croesus thought that was the reason."

"Croesus was her lover, wasn't he? How did he feel about being thrown out?"

"He didn't mind. He was dependent on her, not jealous of her. At least that's my impression."

"When we found Croesus in your apartment," said Severus casually, "we asked him where you were and he refused to tell us. Why would he do that? Why should he keep your where-abouts a secret?"

"Why should he tell you?" countered Timotheus. "We're friends. He has no interest in helping the Roman authorities find me. If a Roman court is interested in me, it probably can't be any good for me. He knows that. Why should he tell you where I am. If you want to find me, do it yourself. That's what he would think."

"He also refused to tell us anything about Fabia, where she was, for instance. Why would he do that?"

"Why should he tell you where she was? Why should he tell you anything about his owner? Especially when she's in the midst of an affair. Suppose she found out that he told Roman authorities where she was? What would happen to him then? She would have him tortured as punishment or sell him. Right now, he's kept in an apartment and has almost no work to do. Occasionally he has to satisfy Fabia in bed. Things could be much worse for a slave than that."

Severus leaned back on the grass, placed his hands behind his head and smiled at the sun. "It's so peaceful here, Vulso," he said. "Peaceful and calm. Timotheus, as a philosopher you can appreciate that, can't you? You're a peaceful man, aren't you?"

Vulso picked up his ears. He was familiar enough with lawyer's tricks to see what was coming. He hoped Timotheus wasn't, but doubted it.

"It is my philosophy," professed Timotheus. Peacefulness, *ataraxia*, the Greeks call it. Calmness, freedom from passion. I teach it to Ferox."

Severus smiled at him. "And you live by your philosophy, don't you? You're not one of those philosophers who advocate one thing and practice another. If you say you're calm and free from passion, then you are that way. Am I right, Timotheus?"

"That's right, *eminentissime*. I am not a man of violence. I do not approve of it. I do not resort to it."

"You're sure about that, Timotheus?"

"Absolutely!" the interjection was emphatic, as if prompted by a disparaging insinuation.

Severus sat up. "Then why did you have the gladiator Taurus beat up a philosopher named Straton in the Subura two days ago?"

Timotheus was fast. "I never did any such thing." His tone suggested that Severus had insulted him by even formulating the question. "I know the incident you're referring to, however. One of Taurus' slaves came to me when I happened to be in my apartment and asked if I knew a Greek philosopher named Straton. I said I didn't. That was all. I never had him beaten up, if he was beaten up."

"He was beaten up. And we know that Taurus did it as a favor to you."

"Did Taurus say that? If he did, he's a liar. How can you take the word of a common ex-gladiator anyway? He said I ordered this Straton beaten up to take the guilt off himself. It's just like him to pretend to be nothing but a tool, when everyone in the Subura knows his reputation – a criminal, the head of a gang. I didn't tell him to beat up anyone and you need more than the word of a scoundrel like him to prove otherwise."

He could talk his way out of anything, thought Vulso. No wonder he was a Greek philosopher. He wasn't just bombast. He was also ingratiating and clever. If he couldn't deceive you one way, he would try another. Vulso began to wish that the judge would let him take Timotheus over the hill for a more forceful interview. Severus, however, switched to another subject.

"I know that you were one of Fabia's lovers." There was no pretense of friendliness anymore. Timotheus hesitated, as if trying to figure out whether to admit it or not.

"Only for a short time," he allowed. "I prefer being Ferox' philosopher to her tool. It's less demanding. Besides I'm a philosopher by trade and not a gigolo."

"Where were you on the seventh and sixth days before the Ides?"

"Let me see. I was here until the eighth day before the Ides. Then I returned to Rome for a few days."

"Do you know who killed Fabia?" asked Severus.

"I don't know that she's dead."

"She's dead."

"I don't believe you."

"It's true. She and her lover were murdered in Croesus' apartment. The body of her lover was dumped on the steps of the Temple of Mars the Avenger."

Timotheus appeared shocked. "When did it happen?" he asked finally.

"Probably on the night of the sixth day before the Ides."

"I didn't do it. I was in my apartment, with Croesus."

"Ferox said you would appreciate an irony in Fabia's murder. Do you?"

"No. Although Ferox would. They were cruel to each other. Romans, your honor, can be very cruel."

He was not challenged on his observation.

"Do you know who murdered Fabia?" asked the judge.

Timotheus reflected awhile. Severus stared at him. Vulso chewed a blade of grass. "As you yourself appreciated, *eminentissime*," he said at last, assuming a philosopher's air, "I am a man of peace and calm. *Ataraxia.* I don't know anything about violence and murder. I can't be of any help to you. For all I know it could have been a burglar. There's so much crime in Rome. It might have been a burglar."

"Could Ferox have done it?"

Timotheus inclined his head. "As I said, *eminentissime*, a burglar."

Severus thought about telling Vulso to take him over the hill, but realized it wouldn't do any good. Timotheus may not have been a philosopher with a fancy reputation and a large income, but he knew his way around and couldn't be easily intimidated.

"Go back to the house," Severus told Timotheus. The philosopher rose and left without a word. Severus and Vulso remained seated on the grass, staring after him. Vulso stuck his middle finger in the air in an obscene gesture.

Severus gave a little laugh. "The one thing it couldn't be," he said, "is burglars."

"Why not?" asked Vulso.

"Burglars aren't in the habit of locking the door when they leave. You had to break down Croesus' door this morning, remember? So it had to be someone with an extra key or someone who could readily induce Fabia to let him into her love nest by simply opening the door. In either case, probably someone she knew. Besides, nothing seemed to be missing; everything seemed to be broken. Murder was the motive. Burglars are out of the question." He rose and picked up his toga. "But I'm sure Timotheus knows that."

"He also lied about the Straton incident," said Vulso, getting up at the same time as the judge.

"Yes." He gave the centurion his toga to carry. "However, what really concerns me now is not so much the outright lies people have told us, but the unspoken ones. In particular, I have a theory that someone concealed a crucial fact from me – a fact that changes everything." He gave the centurion a broad smile. "Today I have deduced what that fact is and who concealed it from me."

THE IDES

XXII

STRATON REPORTS ON
HIS MISSION

All through the pre-dawn hours, citizens and foreign-
ers, freedmen and slaves – the populace of Rome
– poured out of their homes and apartment houses and
streamed singly, in families, and in groups through the
still dark streets, converging from every direction on the
Circus Maximus. At the same time, 20,000 armed men
– seven cohorts of the *Vigiles*, four Urban cohorts and
nine cohorts of the Praetorian Guard – began to fan out
to protect the City from thieves and burglars.

By dawn, well before the presiding government offi-
cials would throw down the white napkin, the arcades of
the huge oblong hippodrome were noisy with the calls of
vendors selling food, bookmakers soliciting bets, pros-
titutes seeking customers, astrologers predicting race
results and magicians selling spells and charms. Slaves
began preparing the track with strong perfumes, special
sand imported from the Egyptian desert and sparkling
grains of mica. The sun turned the race course into a
shimmering metallic band; the stands continuously

filled with eager and impassioned fans; and the stadium
jumped with anticipation and magnetic excitement.

Though still at home, Severus was feeling some of
that excitement coming up from the City. With a reserved
seat in the first fourteen rows because of his upper class
status, he could afford to be more leisurely about his
attendance. He had, however, allowed his slaves to leave
much earlier so they could find good seats. Only Artemisia, who was going to the races with him, and Alexander, joined him for a small cheese and olive breakfast.
Afterwards Alexander would take the children and the
dog to the park for the day. The children had wanted to
go to the races – some of their friends would be going –
but Artemisia flatly refused. They were seven and five-
years-old, too young for the horror of the crashes, she
insisted. Severus was inclined to agree, having himself
been taken by his father to the chariots and the gladiators
when he was their age and had nightmares as a result.
But he was a sports fan nonetheless.

Severus was dressed formally for the races in a toga
and over it he wore a red mantle to show support for
his favorite Red team. He was loyal to the team of his
childhood hero, Diocles, who he argued was the greatest driver in history. Severus still knew his statistics by
heart – among them 1,462 wins with 502 of them coming from behind in the last lap; 35,863,120 sestereces
won. If he ever forgot he could just consult the statue
of Diocles outside the Circus with his racing career and
detailed records in over 20 categories inscribed in stone.

Artemisia purposely dressed in a pale brown *palla*
to show that she rooted for none of the factions, neither

Reds, Green, Blues nor Whites. She usually voiced dis-
interest in the races, sometimes even hostility, but when
actually at the Circus she always got caught up in the
spectacle and the excitement, just like any other fan.
Severus often commented to her about this paradox, but
it didn't disturb her at all. She didn't believe there was
any paradox.

However the breakfast conversation did not concern
chariots. The judge was recounting for his wife and his
librarian the details of the interviews the day before.
Late at night a message from Straton advised him that
shortly after he and Vulso left Ferox' villa, Timotheus
returned to Rome. Straton, lurking by the roadside, had
driven him to the Flaminian Gate, from where he was
followed to his Subura apartment.

"What is he up to?" asked Artemisia.

"I don't know. But I'm sure he knows something.
We'll just have to wait and see."

They didn't have to wait long. Before breakfast was
done Straton arrived in person at Severus' apartment.
Timotheus, he announced, was at the Circus Maximus.
"Two court slaves followed him in. They're probably
sitting near him now. It looks like he intends to spend
the entire day at the chariot races."

"That's all?" said Severus in disappointment. "He
just went to the Circus?"

"That's right. When he arrived in the Subura last
night he first spoke to a grocer across the street and then
to his apartment house porter. Our court slaves watched
the entrance all night. He didn't come out until early this
morning. He again spoke to the doorman and then to the

same grocer. The grocer and a young boy, probably his son, then went with Timotheus to the Circus. They're in the stands now and they have lunch bags with them."

"Curious," remarked Severus.   He thought for a while.   "Yesterday when you drove him from the villa to the City, how did he seem?"

"He seemed to be in a hurry.   He offered to help me fix the wheel in return for a fast ride back to Rome, but once we were under way he changed his mind and told me I could drive leisurely.   We had a pleasant conversation, actually."

Alexander handed Straton a plate with cheese and olives.   He thanked him, ate an olive, and continued his account.

"He asked how long I had been a coachman, whether I regularly drove the Via Flaminia, where I came from — you know, general conversation.   He even told me his name.   I told him mine was Philippus, by the way.   He also gave me a philosophic riddle to puzzle over.   I'm still trying to figure it out."

"What was it?" asked Alexander.

"He asked if I could solve this sophistry — 'when I lie and admit that I lie, do I lie or speak the truth'?"

"Oh, that one," said Severus.

"You know it?"

"When I was studying in Athens the Roman students used to gather together for the Saturnalia holidays before the New Year, and for amusement we would sometimes challenge each other with little riddles and puzzles. Whoever solved one would win a small prize, a laurel crown or a book.   I even remember that riddle being asked."

"What's the answer?"

"I think," offered Alexander, "the accepted answer is that 'I speak the truth when I admit I lied.'"

"It's not important," said Severus. "What is important is Timotheus. I thought he knew something about the murders and then, when he left the villa in a hurry, I was sure he would do something because of his knowledge. But now..." He trailed off into thought until Artemisia reminded him that they had to leave for the Circus.

Severus snapped out of his reverie with a smile. Then he and Artemisia went to join a quarter of a million spectators to revel in Rome's grandest and most enjoyable public spectacle – a full day at the chariot races in the magnificent Circus Maximus: 24 thrilling races, opening with a colorful parade of charioteers and musicians and closing with a free State banquet for everyone.

XXIII

SEVERUS GOES TO THE CIRCUS MAXIMUS AND IS CALLED AWAY

The first race was a classic. It would be talked about in Rome for days, maybe weeks. It was filled with close calls, spills, comebacks, dramatic changes in the lead, and daring driving — exactly what the crowd had come to see. In the end it had come down to a confrontation between the two factions with the largest followings in Rome, the Greens and the Blues. The final dash for the white line had set the fans boiling with emotion. Even Severus, whose Red team had "shipwrecked" with the White chariot on the sixth lap, was moved by the excitement of the seventh and final lap to temporarily switch his allegiance to the Blues.

It was, however, the Green charioteer who threw up his right arm and it was the strip of green cloth that the herald held up to signal the winner. The groans and curses of the Blue fans were drowned out by a wild cheer from the more numerous Greens, accompanied by the furious waving of green banners and cloths throughout the stadium. At the same time, flocks of green-dyed pigeons were released from the stands by gamblers to notify other gamblers outside the stadium and the City of the results of the important first race.

The victorious charioteer saluted the President of the Games in his box and received the palm leaf victory crown from his hands. Later the driver and owners of the Greens would split the 50,000 sesterces first prize. To renewed cheering and chants of *euge! euge!* – very good! very good! – the charioteer saluted the two co-heirs to the throne in the Imperial Box. The younger of the Caesars, Lucius Verus, a devotee of the Greens, waved back enthusiastically. The other Caesar, Marcus Aurelius, barely looked up from his book. The victor then circled the hippodrome in triumph to the accompaniment of the music of trumpets and hydraulic organ, while cheers, kisses, flowers and presents poured down on him from each section of the stands as he passed by.

Severus and Artemisia resumed their seats while most of the crowd was still standing and cheering.

"How much did we lose on this one?" asked Artemisia.

"100 sesterces."

"And only 23 races to go," she laughed.

"Don't worry. I have a tip from Vulso on the 17th race."

"What does he say?"

"You know his tips. He'll never say anything positively. It's always just a rumor. Well, the 'rumor' this time is that the trace horse for the Greens in that race – they're the favorites – may not be feeling too well.

Something in his fodder. I don't know how he gets his information – maybe from stable hands, trainers or gamblers – but he's usually reliable. He suggested we bet on the Blues to win in the 17th."

They began studying their racing form, ignoring the acrobats and trick riders who had come out on the track to amuse the crowd until the next race. Both he and his wife attacked the supply of chickpeas they had bought on the way into the stadium from the vendors under the arcades.

"I think we should take the Reds," suggested Severus. "Fifty sesterces."

Artemisia agreed and Severus signalled to one of the many bookmakers running up and down the aisles taking bets. Much of the crowd had by now placed their bets and began to take up the rhythmic chant, "The others! The others!" to show they had recovered from one race and wanted the next one to begin.

Shortly before the trumpets sounded the call, a messenger elbowed his way across the row and gave the judge a wax tablet. Severus noted the court's seal as he undid the threads.

"It's from Proculus," he said to Artemisia. "He's also sent for Vulso and Straton."

"What happened?" she asked.

"Phryne. She's returned and right now is at Ferox' house in the City."

He took a stylus from a writing case the slave held out to him and erased Proculus' message with the broad flat end of the instrument. With the pointed end he wrote a reply on the smoothed wax surface, reclosed the threads, and gave the tablet back to the messenger who immediately departed.

"I'll have to go," he told Artemisia with a mixture of disappointment and anticipation. "I instructed Proculus to have everyone meet me at Ferox' house as soon as possible."

"It can't wait?" said Artemisia hopefully.

"I'm afraid not. I was expecting something like this to happen. I was hoping it wouldn't be today."

"I can sit with my friend Valeria and her husband a few rows back," she said understandingly. Artemisia snatched the racing form from Severus and smiled at him as they rose. "And while you're gone, I intend to win back that 100 sesterces."

When he left the stadium the judge strode through the crowd of litter-bearers, oblivious to their entreaties to hire them. Neither did he notice the emptiness of the city streets outside the hubbub of the Circus Maximus. He was lost in thought, his hands clasped behind his back, his head slightly bowed. Some hidden resource alone kept him going in the right direction. He was considering what the return of Phryne meant. Had she been at the scene of the murder itself? Had she seen who had done it and run away in fear? What would she know?

Two blocks before reaching the Ferox mansion the judge's posture suddenly shifted. He stood up straight and looked around to see where he was. A smile played over his face and eyes and he quickened his pace. One block before reaching the house he stopped in his tracks. A feeling of fear passed through him and he began to run.

Menelaus, the slave in charge of Ferox' household, let Severus in. He looked as haggard as on the day he had appeared in the courtroom.

"*Eminentissime*," he said respectfully, "your clerk is already here. The centurion also. Phryne is in her room. She is very distraught. It's terrible."

Severus questioned Menelaus in the vestibule, just inside the door. "When did she return?"

"Shortly after the first hour. She was brought here by a priest of the Temple of Isis, *eminentissime*. I have his name for you."

"Is that where she was all this time? At a Temple of Isis?"

"Yes, but she's very frightened. She won't tell me what happened. Won't tell anyone. She says she will only speak to the authorities." He looked apologetic. "It took my messengers a long time to find you and your staff, *eminentissime*."

Severus started walking into the interior of the house. "Where is my clerk?"

Menelaus showed him through the atrium to the *tablinum*. Severus dismissed the slave and entered alone. Proculus was pacing the floor nervously.

"Judge," he exclaimed when he saw Severus. "I'm glad you're here. Vulso is guarding her door — off the peristyle."

"How did you find out about this?"

"I was home, fortunately. Menelaus sent a messenger to the court. Someone at the court sent a messenger to my apartment. I know where your seat is in the Circus, of course. I went to get Vulso myself." He dropped his voice. "I found him at home and with two naked women. Please speak to him, sir," the clerk implored. "He introduced me as a procurer for high class orgies who had come to look them over. While he was getting dressed they put on the most obscene performance I ever..."

"All right," said Severus, trying to keep a straight face. "I'll talk to him. Did you get my message to bring slaves from the court?"

"Yes, judge. There was only a skeleton staff available, but I managed to get a squad of ten together. They're on their way here."

The judge called Menelaus back and asked to be taken to see Phryne. Menelaus escorted him to a small room where she was waiting. Vulso, guarding the door, saluted the judge and barred the way to the slave, closing the door behind Severus.

Phryne was seated on a stool and looked up at him when he entered. Severus was struck by her beauty. The painting the police artist had made hadn't done her complete justice. Her face was soft and her lips sensual, her eyes a cat-like and vivid green. Her loose brown tunic did not entirely hide the curves of her body. Though there was a haunted look about her at the moment, it did not detract from her appeal; instead it evoked a desire to protect. Severus sat down on a stool next to her, introduced himself and spoke in a consoling tone.

"Where have you been all this time, Phryne?"

"At a Temple of Isis, *eminentissime*." Her voice was soft and appealing. "Outside the City. I was afraid and sought sanctuary there."

"Why were you afraid?"

"I saw two murders, *eminentissime*."

"Tell me about them."

"I cannot." She looked at him imploringly. "It concerns my master and my mistress. I may not testify about them. I am only a slave."

"This is not a court, Phryne. There is no stenographer here and there is no statue of Jupiter Fidius. What you tell me is not testimony. We are merely having a private conversation. Besides, I am a judge of Rome and I command you to tell me." His voice was soothing, but firm.

"I saw my mistress murdered, *eminentissime*. And her friend also."

"Tell me everything that happened, from the time you left this house with Fabia until now."

Phryne composed herself. "My mistress ordered me to accompany her out after the siesta. Then she gave me an errand to do. I was to go to a hotel, called Athena's Mantle, near the Ostia gate, and find a man named Anaximander there. I was to bring him to Fabia. She had gone to a secret apartment she had near the wooden statue of Vertumnus, on the Vicus Tuscus. She gave me the address. I did as my mistress commanded."

Phryne buried her face in her hands. A look of fear was in her eyes when she looked up again. "It was on the second night we were there when it happened. It was so sudden, so frightening. I am still in a daze when I think about it." Distress was in her voice. "I heard a commotion and then the door burst open. I saw my master and four men rush in with drawn swords and knives. My mistress died quickly. Anaximander tried to fight, but was cut down." She rocked back and forth, wringing her hands together. "He was only wounded at first, but they followed him around the apartment, hacking at him, until he died. It was horrible. I cowered in a corner, afraid they would kill me too."

"But my master then came and stood in front of me, his sword dripping with blood. He had a strange, almost satisfied smile on his face. I thought he was going to kill me. But instead he told me not to worry; I was to be spared. He said he had nothing against me. It was Fabia he hated. He said that as his slave I couldn't testify against him anyway, so I could go. But he ordered me to run away and leave the City and never return.

"I didn't know what to do, but I got out of there as quickly as possible. My master and his men were busy wrapping the bodies in cloaks. I wandered around in confusion, not knowing where I was going, what I was to do. I found myself on a road leading out of the City. Then I became tired and thirsty. I had to stop somewhere. I saw a Temple of Isis and asked for refuge there. The priests were kind enough to help me. They let me stay a few days, but they said I would have to leave, that they could not harbor a runaway slave. After a while, after I had calmed down, they convinced me it would be best to return home. This morning one of the priests brought me here."

"I see," said Severus. He got up, opened the door and spoke to the centurion. "Vulso, as fast as possible — commandeer a chariot from the Imperial Post if you have to — go to Ferox' villa and arrest him."

"On what charge?"

"Murder," snapped the Severus.

Vulso saluted and left, while Severus called for Proculus. "Quintus, send a court-slave to the Circus with a note..." He stopped to wait for Proculus to open a tablet and take down what he dictated. "...to the Urban Prefect. He's in his box at the Circus. Tell him that Phryne has returned with an explanation of what happened to Fabia and Anaximander. Ask him to come to my apartment at the first hour tonight. Say it's urgent he attend. Use my personal seal on the tablet for him." He took off his ring with a carving of a trireme and handed it to his clerk. "Send another slave to the Circus to find Artemisia and Flaccus and ask them to come home, also by the first night hour. Then send a slave to find Straton and Alexander. They're spending the day together with the children and the dog. I think they went to the Gardens of Lucullus or the Gardens of Sallust. I know Alexander likes the library in the former and the area around the obelisk in the latter. Make sure they come home by the same time."

Proculus finished scribbling his shorthand and went to find slaves to carry the messages, while Severus returned to question Phryne more closely.

XXIV

VULSO RETURNS FROM THE VILLA

When the bronze bird on the water clock chirped the first night hour, only Alexander, Straton, Proculus and Severus were there to hear it. Artemisia and Flaccus had acknowledged the judge's message and were expected back momentarily. The Urban Prefect had replied that he wouldn't be able to come until the third night hour: he had to attend the opening ceremony of the State feast and dine with the Senate on the Capitoline Hill. Vulso had not yet returned from his mission.

There was little food in the house and no slaves to serve it. They were all at the public banquet and Alexander was not expected to fill in for them. He did, however, light the oil lamps and then settled down in the library to a game of *tabula* with Straton. Proculus strolled about, casually inspecting the books and art works. He particularly admired a bronze eagle perched on a table. "Look how every feather is done down to the last detail," he commented.

"It's exquisite, isn't it," said Severus as he tied a red leather thong through his hair. "Artemisia found it in an antique store in the Subura."

Severus had changed into a comfortable white tunic with a gold olive branch pattern embroidered inside the red *clavi* and wore equally comfortable wool-lined house slippers. He sat on the edge of a reading couch, tuning his seven-stringed lyre and striking random chords with a plectrum. He had kept up his music since learning it in school as a boy. He liked playing duets with Artemisia on the double flute and sometimes they would join friends to play in an amateur orchestra. Pulling the lyre strap over his shoulder, he stood up and strummed an emotional song in the Phrygian mode.

"I'm a secret admirer of Nero," he said to his clerk when he finished the piece. "He was an excellent lyre player, you know."

Proculus looked slightly scandalized, as Severus knew he would. "Judge!" he protested. "How can you say that? Nero was irresponsible and extravagant, not the least bit conscientious or devoted to duty like our modern emperors. If it weren't for the civil service Nero might have ruined the empire."

"True. But he was by nature a temperamental artist. He thought the empire should be entertained during his reign, rather than governed. That's why his memory is still honored by the Greeks and the Roman mob. But you're right, of course. He was more suited to be a musician than an emperor, though with the help of Seneca he did give Rome five good years before he went crazy." Upon which, moodily, he strummed another song in the Phrygian mode.

The music cloaked Severus' anxiety as he waited for Vulso's return from the villa. It also encouraged a sense of balance and harmony within himself. This was now important because his mind was racing furiously. The solution to the case was at hand. But he felt no elation. Far from it. He felt fear, almost panic, for what lay ahead. What was he to do? Severus ran it through his mind again. Two solutions seemed to fit the facts. One was quite pleasing; everyone would be satisfied by the outcome. But he knew this solution to be false. The truthful solution, the one that engendered dread, involved a moral catastrophe. Was it possible that the false solution was morally desirable, though legally unjust, while the truth served justice, but offended morality? What would a philosopher-king do? He could not step out of the case as in the example that he had challenged his assessor with a few days before, where the judge could not decide between the dishonest man and the honest man who had no proof. No, he would have to make a judgment, one way or the other. So Severus would have to draw on everything inside himself, on his character and his learning, his philosophy and his emotions, on his sense of life and its meaning. He switched to a song in the plaintive Lydian mode to calm himself and induce a state of meditation. The case was solved. It was whether to reveal the solution, it occurred to him, that was the real problem.

Vulso returned a few minutes before the twelfth hour. Alexander let him in. He stalked directly into the library where Severus, Artemisia, Straton, Flaccus and Proculus were waiting. The centurion had a scroll clutched tightly in his hand. He took off his helmet, wiped the sweat of travel from his face, and looked directly at the judge.

"Ferox is dead! He committed suicide! His body was still warm when I got there. He drank hemlock, like Socrates." Vulso held out the scroll. "He left a confession, admitting that he murdered both Fabia and Anaximander." He handed the scroll to the judge. "It says he buried Fabia under that plane tree – where we interviewed Timotheus."

Severus unfurled the scroll, read it, and then handed it to Artemisia, while the others read it over her shoulder.

"That clinches it," commented Alexander quickly. "His story is the same as Phryne's."

"Congratulations," offered Proculus to the judge. "You have brought about a quick solution to a difficult case."

Severus took a deep breath and let it out; it was as much a sigh as a relief of tension. "No one," he said, "would be more pleased than I to conclude that Ferox killed himself out of remorse for murdering Fabia and Anaximander. Well, almost no one. The exception is the actual killer."

"What are you saying?" exclaimed three people at once.

"Everything is wrapped up," urged Alexander above the commotion. "The suicide, the confession, Phryne's story, the location of Fabia's body. What's left unexplained or unaccounted for?"

Several others agreed with him.

"I said yesterday," replied Severus in an almost argumentative tone, "that I had a theory that someone concealed an important fact from me. The concealed fact was that Phryne was alive; I deduced it from the evidence and our observations. But it was only a theory until she reappeared today. Now it is no longer theoretical. Someone else connected with the case must have known she was alive all along, but couldn't reveal it without giving himself away. No, my friends, Phryne's story and Ferox' confession are both false. Ferox didn't commit suicide. He was murdered, just like his wife and her lover."

"And you know who did it?" asked Alexander.

"Yes. I do."

"Who is it?"

"Don't you know?" asked Severus, looking first at Alexander, then at his wife, and then at the others one at a time.

They all returned uncomprehending looks, either from lack of knowledge or deliberately hiding their suspicions. No one wanted to face the truth.

THE NIGHT OF THE IDES

XXV

A SYMPOSIUM ON MURDER

The oil lamps in Severus' dining room evoked the eerie glow common to nighttime gatherings. The judge and his wife reclined on the host's couch. The Urban Prefect reclined in the 'consul's post', the guest of honor's place opposite the host. Next to him were Flaccus and Vulso, while a third divan held Proculus, Straton and Alexander. The square dining table between the couches had eight individual platters, each with a selection of cold banquet food brought back from the public feast. Each one had an assortment of patties: oyster patties, mussel patties, fish patties and sow udder patties; and a helping of thrush on asparagus and eggs. Slaves, some of them tipsy from the feast, stood against the frescoed walls preparing kraters of wine on a sideboard, ready to fill a cup whenever it became empty. Everyone wore garlands of roses or violets round their necks, as was customary for a symposium. Now and then yells, cheers and drunken songs of revellers penetrated the walls from the street below.

The symposium began with the traditional ceremony. One slave carried in the small statues of the Severus family *lares*, the ancestral guardian spirits of the household, while another slave brought a smoking brazier to the master of the house. Severus sprinkled a small amount of grain, salt and wine on the fire, making the brazier sizzle and smoke. The slave solemnly intoned "the gods are propitious" and everyone observed a moment's silence. Then the gods were taken out of the room.

"I should begin," said Severus, "by telling you how I figured out what happened. How I know, for instance, that Phryne's story and Ferox' confession are equally false." He looked over at the guests.

"It all comes back to the character of Fabia and how she would have arranged the first meeting in seventeen years with her lover Anaximander. By focusing on this question I first suspected Croesus' apartment was the murder scene. But now, consider what their meeting would have been like. Who would have been there? Clearly it would have been a romantic tryst. Private and intimate. If that's true, what was Phryne doing with Fabia and Anaximander? Why was she in the apartment with them the first night or the next, as she claims?"

"That praetorian, Metellus," Vulso suggested, "thought that Fabia and Phryne were sleeping together. Maybe this was a three-way affair." He didn't sound convinced.

"Does that make sense?" asked Severus. Remember, Fabia was reconstructing this scene from the past. A small apartment in Ephesus. Romantic, intimate, two young lovers alone. Where does Phryne fit into it? She wasn't even in Ephesus. So why should she participate in the reunion?"

Straton joined in. "Phryne stayed there as a slave. She attended to their needs."

"What needs?" said the judge. "We found the apartment fully supplied with food, water, wine and all sorts of provisions. It was planned that way. Croesus was specifically told to stock the apartment and leave. There was enough for at least a week. They didn't need Phryne there at all. Even more importantly, consider the size of the apartment. Where would Phryne be during this passionate reunion between Fabia and Anaximander? In the next room? With no door? Surely not. She would only be an intruder." He paused for a sip of wine. "One of the reasons I was so anxious to find the love nest was just to see the size of the apartment. I wanted to ascertain whether there was a separate room for Phryne, where she could be out of the way. But Croesus' apartment did not permit such an arrangement. It was too small. There was simply no place for Phryne."

"But then," joined in Flaccus, "her presence doesn't make sense. She shouldn't have been there."

"Exactly."

"So then how do you explain her presence?" asked the Urban Prefect.

"It can't be explained," said Severus.

Flaccus clapped his hands and gave a little laugh. He got the idea. The judge looked around. No one else seemed the wiser.

"If Phryne couldn't have been there," he said finally, "then obviously she wasn't there. After escorting Anaximander to the apartment building and telling him which apartment Fabia was in, she got off the stage. In no way could she have seen Ferox kill the two lovers because she wasn't in the right place at the right time. And if she wasn't there, where was she? She couldn't have fled in fear to the Temple of Isis: there had been no murders as yet."

"Then where did she go?" asked two people at once.

"Where could she go? Where would one expect a slave to go after finishing an errand?" asked Severus in turn.

"Home, I suppose," chanced Straton.

"Of course. If Fabia had no more use for her, she would have sent her home. Isn't that obvious?"

"Then why didn't someone tell us?" wondered Proculus.

"Exactly. Why didn't one of the slaves in Ferox' house tell us that she had returned home after having left Fabia? Why had someone concealed that fact? For one of the slaves certainly knew. Remember, the procedure in that house was for a slave, when returning from an errand, to report directly to Menelaus, the chief household slave. So why did Menelaus conceal the fact that Phryne had returned? Moreover," continued Severus, "if Menelaus knew that Phryne had returned, he also must have known that Fabia had not disappeared. So if Menelaus knew no one was missing, whey did he go to the Urban Prefect the next day and tell him that both Fabia and Phryne could not be found?"

"Is Menelaus behind the murders?" ventured the prefect incredulously.

"It has to be him. And Phryne must have been one of his accomplices. Of course, they couldn't have done it alone. Menelaus is too old. Phryne is not strong enough. There must have been other accomplices to help with the actual stabbings. But there is no doubt that Menelaus and Phryne are among the murderers."

No one said anything. All eyes were on Severus who helped himself to an oyster patty. Finally Alexander asked who, in the judge's view, were the other murderers? There was a slight tremor in his voice. "What about Timotheus, Croesus, even Ferox?"

"We can eliminate Senator Ferox," replied Severus, "since Menelaus and Phryne contrived to blame him for murdering his wife and her lover and then killed him as part of their plan. Far from being an accessory to the crime, he is one of the victims, along with Fabia."

"Then why did you send me out to arrest him at his villa?" asked Vulso.

"When Phryne returned she implicated Ferox. I sent you to take him into custody in a forlorn attempt to save his life, not because I thought he was guilty."

"That leaves Timotheus and Croesus?" said Alexander. "That so-called philosopher had Straton beaten up. He's in league with a gang of criminals and he stands to gain in Ferox' will."

"And Croesus also seems guilty to me," interjected the prefect. "The murders occurred in his apartment. He was one of Fabia's lovers. And he was a good friend of Timotheus."

"And Timotheus claimed," added Vulso, "that he and Croesus were together in his apartment the night Fabia was murdered."

"Let's start with Timotheus," said the judge. "Proculus, you've been around the criminal courts for many years. You've seen many cases. Did you ever hear of one where a murderer, trying to conceal his guilt, puts the investigating judge on the trail of his accomplices? Don't bother to answer: the question is purely rhetorical. So, when one of the murderers, Menelaus, put us on the trail of Timotheus and Croesus as lovers of Fabia, the lesson is they are not his accomplices."

"That would be a reasonable presumption, judge, although it is surely not conclusive."

"Still, what actual proof do we have that Timotheus is guilty? Straton's black eye? Straton walked into a gang of criminals in the Subura, but that's no proof that they committed these murders."

Flaccus couldn't contain himself. "Even assuming that Straton's encounter with the gladiator is unrelated to the murders, why did Timotheus leave Ferox' villa in a hurry? His departure was related to the murder of Ferox, wasn't it? He left yesterday and this morning Ferox dies. In my opinion, he left because he knew Ferox was going to be murdered and wanted to be somewhere else?"

"Granted. But the question is whether Timotheus knew Ferox would be killed because he was one of the killers or because he figured out who was going to kill Ferox and might not want to be in the way when it happened."

"How can you tell which?" asked Flaccus. "The facts are consistent with both innocence and guilt. Timotheus would have left the villa in either case."

"That's not exactly correct. I'm certain he was innocent of the murder of Fabia. And if he was innocent of killing her, he was undoubtedly not part of the conspiracy and thus also innocent of the murder of Ferox."

"How do you know he didn't take part in the murder of Fabia?" asked three people at once.

"Because he has a good alibi."

"What do mean 'alibi'!" exclaimed Vulso. "You don't believe that story he made up about being in his apartment with Croesus, do you? He just said that on the spur of the moment."

"On the contrary. It's just because he didn't make it up that I do believe him. Let's look at it this way. Timotheus knows that Ferox is going to be killed and he wants out. What does he do? He constructs an elaborate alibi from the moment he leaves the villa. First he takes a coach back to the City and tells the driver he can take his time. Then he has a conversation in which he tells the driver his name and finds out the driver's name and the route he usually travels. Then he gives the driver a riddle he can hardly forget. So if he's ever asked about when he left the villa, Timotheus can give us the name of the coachman who took him to Rome and the coachman will corroborate it. He'll remember Timotheus and his riddle."

"I wondered what that was all about," remarked Straton.

"But he doesn't stop there. He goes to his apartment and makes sure to talk to the grocer across the street and the house porter. The porter will have seen him enter and could testify that Timotheus was there all night. Moreover, Timotheus also arranges with his grocer to spend the next day with him in the Circus Maximus, amid a quarter of a million people. What better alibi is there than that?"

"But you're just telling us how good his alibi is for the murder of Ferox," insisted Straton. "The alibi he gave for the murder of Fabia is unprovable. He relies on a slave who himself has a motive to kill Fabia."

"It's the contrast," said Severus forcefully. "Is 'Croesus' the type of alibi Timotheus would construct if he needed one? Were he part of the plan to kill Fabia, don't you think he would have fabricated an alibi like the one he constructed for the death of Ferox? Couldn't he have had the gladiator Taurus and some of his associates say he had been in the taverna, for instance? That would be simple enough. Anything would have been better than being alone in his apartment with Croesus."

Alexander concurred. "Timotheus is too wily, Straton, to have left himself without an alibi for such an event if he had a hand in it. In this case, the very meagerness of his story is proof of its truth. He wasn't part of the plot to kill Fabia; therefore, he wasn't part of the plot to kill Ferox. He must have guessed who killed her and what was going to happen next." He looked dejected. "I suppose he decided to let Ferox die to collect his inheritance. That's why he didn't tell the judge that Ferox' life was in danger. He wasn't a true philosopher."

"Maybe not. But clever," said Vulso. "We'll never be able to prove that he went to the Circus Maximus to set up an alibi, that he knew Ferox was going to die. He'll just say he is a fan of the chariot races, and that's that."

"There's one thing I don't understand," said the prefect. "If Timotheus has an alibi in Croesus, then Croesus has an alibi in Timotheus, doesn't he?"

"That's right."

"You mean Croesus is innocent too?"

"That's right," repeated Severus.

"Then why didn't he talk under torture?" broke in Vulso. "Why did he claim he was a free man and a citizen? Why did he try to run away from me?"

"It couldn't be to avoid being pushed around by you, could it?" sneered Straton. "Your manner is so ingratiating. He should have been overjoyed to accompany you to a Roman courtroom. He..."

"We get the point, Straton," interrupted Severus. "Yes, Croesus is innocent. Not only because of the alibi, but the presumption is stronger in his case. Menelaus willingly put us on his trail. He must have known that if we subjected him to judicial torture there would be nothing to worry about."

"Anyway," interjected the prefect, "he falsely claimed he was a free man and a citizen. That's a crime. He'll pay for that at least."

Severus stood up. "Right now, I think we should all take a break, wash up, make room for some more wine and stretch our legs. Afterwards, I'll reconstruct the crime for you: who else did it, why it was done and how it was carried out."

"Who else did it?" asked the prefect when everyone had freshened up and was resettled on their couch with wine and fruit on the table.

"Other slaves in the Ferox *familia*," said Severus.

"All of them?"

"Menelaus and Phryne, certainly. One or more of the four slaves at Ferox' villa poisoned him. Certainly slaves from the city house took part in the murders of Fabia and Anaximander, perhaps all of them. Let me reconstruct it."

The judge drained his glass. A slave refilled it.

"I'll start with the motive. Why would the slave want to kill Fabia and Ferox? To ask the question is to answer it. Why they wouldn't want to be rid of them is a harder question to answer. They were caught between Scylla and Charybdis, between the rock and the whirlpool, between two lunatics who were waging war against each other, and who were using their slaves, sometimes as weapons, sometimes as tools and sometimes as the battleground. Croesus and Phryne are two obvious examples, but not the only ones. Fabia didn't whip them and dress them in rags like her husband, but she humiliated them and used them in ways that must have made them hate her as much as they hated Ferox."

"Besides, there was also a strong practical reason for them to do away with both Fabia and Ferox. It's not easily that slaves can get away with killing their master. They are natural suspects. 'So many slaves, so many enemies,' as the saying goes. If they could kill one and pin the blame on the other, it would solve their problem. It was an open secret that Ferox and Fabia were trying to get rid of each other. So it would be believable that Ferox killed her and then committed suicide in the face of his arrest. It would also exonerate the slaves – so they thought – from suspicion."

"The opportunity to carry out their plan presented itself with the arrival of Anaximander. I don't know how far in advance they knew he was coming. We will find out. But when Phryne returned home after escorting Fabia's lover to Croesus' apartment, she must have informed Menelaus. The slaves must then have realized that the chance they waited for had come."

"So at the appointed time a horde of slaves rushed into the love nest with weapons drawn. Fabia and Anaximander must have fought for their lives in a wild, swirling chase around the apartment. Anaximander was stabbed thirty times, Fabia probably as much. They were assassinated like Caesar on the Ides of March. Poor lovers. Some reunion after seventeen years."

"And how about the bodies?" asked someone.

"That was also part of their design. They would not throw them into the Tiber or leave them in the apartment until the stench made the dogs howl. No. They would use the bodies to implement the second part of the plan — to incriminate Ferox. They loaded the two corpses into a litter and carried them safely through the streets of Rome. Then they dumped Anaximander's body on the steps of the Temple of Mars the Avenger. It would cause a sensation, of course, and suggest vengeance was the motive for the crime. And when the connection was made between Anaximander and Fabia, Ferox would become an immediate suspect."

"How could they be sure of that?" interrupted the prefect. "How could they know that connection would be made?"

"They purposely left the fisherman and queen amulet around Anaximander's neck and his message tablet with the impression from the amulet on Fabia's table. If we hadn't made the connection ourselves, the slaves would have contrived to let us know about it some other way."

"Fabia's remains they took to Ferox' villa and buried in a nearby meadow. It would not be discovered until they were ready — until Ferox' confession told us where to find it."

"Why did they wait before killing Ferox?" inquired Alexander.

"There had to be some time lapse between the slaying of Fabia and Ferox since he was to be cast as the murderer. But I think they waited to kill him until after I interrogated him. They knew Ferox well; they knew he was unbalanced and would give me that impression, as in fact he did. My interview with him would serve to further their plan. After all, he admitted moral responsibility for his wife's death and told us he wished her dead."

"And with the story of Phryne and Ferox' fake confession," acquiesced the prefect, "who could doubt his guilt."

"Yes. Today's events came as the final touch. They poisoned Ferox with hemlock and forged a 'confession.'"

Severus stopped and, somewhat theatrically, let everyone absorb his logic. Then, knowing how to handle his effects, he turned toward his librarian. "Of course," he announced, "our perceptive Alexander will have noticed the flaw in what I have just told you."

Alexander had noticed it. "The flaw is that there is no proof. No evidence. It is pure deduction."

Everyone started shouting at once. The prefect took precedence. "What do you mean, no proof? There's all that evidence that led us to figure it all out."

Severus jerked his head back and raised his palm in a negative gesture. "Alexander is right. What can we present in court. The slaves will have their lawyers. What do we have? Only speculation. Inferences upon inferences." He stood up.

The prefect also stood up. "It hardly matters." said the prefect. "because fortunately the wisdom of our Roman law provides us with a practical answer. So I will take over the case from here and preside at the trial myself." He looked at Proculus. Everyone understood. Alexander covered his eyes.

"Court clerk. You will arrange for the *quaestionarius*. Tomorrow morning.

EPILOGUE

MARCUS FLAVIUS SEVERUS :
TO HIMSELF

When Vulso arrived with several squads of the Urban Cohort to arrest the slaves, they were asleep, exhausted by their celebrations of the night before, when they thought their plan successful, their tormentors dead and their freedom assured. It was. Vulso remarked, like the scene the Greeks found when they stole into Troy from inside the Trojan horse. The Trojans were sleeping the sleep of revelers, oblivious to their destruction.

About a month later, the day of the executions in the arena, and upon the recommendation of the Urban Prefect, the emperor conferred upon me the award of 'The Privileges of the Father of Three Children'. Then at noon the slaves were put to death in the Flavian Amphitheater. All thirty-six of them had confessed their guilt under torture, named accomplices and were tried and sentenced by the Urban Prefect presiding in his own court. All thirty-six were crucified in front of 50,000 roaring spectators, then tortured and while still alive, wild animals tore pieces from their bodies.

The ones I knew best and felt particular sympathy for, Menelaus and Phryne, were among them, of course. But in Rome, the most savage, most gruesome, most merciless punishment fits the most feared crime – slaves murdering masters.

I wasn't there to see it. None of us were, not even Vulso. But we all knew what was happening. I deliberately left the City with Alexander and went to the Gardens of Servilius. I pretended I wanted to see statues: to see the Flora of Praxiteles and the Seated Vesta of Scopas in the Gardens. I didn't want to be in the City when the bloody show took place in the arena. Seneca described it perfectly. Rome for once is quiet, peaceful, almost pastoral. But now and then a "sudden, universal, burst of applause" shakes the City and reverberates among the hills. That sound, Seneca said, that "confused rumbling of the crowd is like the waves, like the wind which whips the forest, like everything which conveys only unintelligible sounds." That day those sounds would have been intelligible to me and I didn't want to hear them.

But even the tranquility and beauty of the gardens and the art couldn't take our thoughts off the case. For the first time I envied the grammarians who are always in the parks on such days, arguing about some obscure point of language, disputing the correct form of the vocative case of some word or other. As usual, we gave their shouting and wrangling a wide berth when we encountered them on the paths or among the trees, but today I longed to join in and devote my mind to such harmless topics.

Alexander asked me about Timotheus. He's a rich man now. Ferox made him his heir. Of course, Ferox intended it as a cruelty. He had no money, except for the value of the slaves he owned and they're all dead. But the catch was that Fabia died first and she left no will. Ferox became her heir before his death and everything then passed to Timotheus. He even inherited Croesus. He's already moved into Ferox' mansion in the City and restocked it. He bought a batch of fifty slaves to start with. How ironic. Fabia had tried to convince her former lover, Publius Planta, to kill Ferox for her. Whether she pushed him off the balcony because he refused, we'll never know. Yet all she had to do was just ask the slaves. They would have obliged with relish.

Alexander chastised me. He lectured me about law and justice. He said I could have "solved" the case with Ferox' confession, Phryne's story and the unearthing of Fabia's body. No one would have questioned Ferox' guilt. He said he thought I could understand the desire of the slaves to be freed from bad masters. He said I should know that they wouldn't murder again, that there was moral justification for what they did. Why did I have to expose them and condemn them to horrible deaths? He even cited a legal precedent from a Greek court. He mentioned the case of a woman from Smyrna. Her husband and son had murdered her other son by a former marriage. So she poisoned them in revenge. The case was referred to the Court of the Areopagus in Athens. The decision was to adjourn the case for 100 years, for the court neither wished to condone the woman's crime — the law would not permit it — nor to punish her for her justifiable offense.

I replied that was a Greek court, not a Roman one. Roman law is inexorable. There is no such thing as a 100-year adjournment in a Roman court. I said, unless a series of very clever lawyers, adept at delaying tactics, could do it. But the record in that regard is 20 years. No, I replied, only the whim of an emperor could grant a 100-year adjournment and our modern emperors rule by laws, not whims. It is considered a virtue, I told him.

Then I admitted to him that I had thought carefully about "solving" the case with Ferox' confession and why I rejected it. I explained that when I was a student in Athens with Calvisius Taurus, we would discuss the reasons for punishing crime. Plato, for instance, had cited two: deterrence and reformation; the one to prevent people from committing crimes, the other to prevent the criminal from persevering. Yet neither of those reasons was the decisive consideration. I agreed it was unlikely the slaves would murder again, though I couldn't be sure, of course. I also acknowledged that exposing the slaves would not be much of a deterrant. There had been similar cases in the past – even famous ones during the reigns of Nero and Hadrian – and there would undoubtedly be similar ones in the future. But Calvisius Taurus, as well as other philosophers, mention a third reason for punishing crime. "To maintain the dignity and prestige of the person sinned against, lest he be dishonored and held in contempt." In other words, to do justice to the victim.

Alexander argued that justice was done to Fabia and Ferox, that I couldn't say they didn't deserve their end, though the means might have been excessive.

I agreed with him. If the slaves had killed just Fabia and Ferox I would have falsified the records and let them off. But what about Anaximander? Are we to forget him? I asked. Did he deserve to die for the baseness of Fabia and Ferox? What did that poor mosaicist do to merit thirty knife wounds? Doesn't he deserve justice? Whey did the slaves slaughter him? That was their crime, as far as I was concerned. I exposed them to avenge the murder of Anaximander. I told my librarian that if the woman from Smyrna had poisoned innocent people, the Court of the Areopagus would have condemned her.

He didn't answer me.

Strange and ironic things sometimes happen, things which are often unexplainable. Someone who believes in the gods would say the slaves doomed themselves by leaving the body of Anaximander on the steps of the Temple of Mars the Avenger. Even those who don't believe in the gods could see an omen, a portent because the planet Mars was the brightest object in the night sky during that whole week. Could Mars then leave such a desecration unanswered? Anaximander's murder would be avenged. And so it came about.

I also told Alexander that I was sorry and that he was free.

I remember how he looked at me. We were seated on a bench. Before us were the Flora and the Seated Vesta; the one, as Lucan said, exuding the intelligent "cool gleam" of a work by Praxiteles, the other the voluptuous forms of a Scopas. He said simply that I didn't have to do it.

I told him I knew it wouldn't correct the balance for all those people, but that I wanted to do it. Call it a whim, I said. Didn't he want to be free.

He said it was his fondest hope. Tears welled in his eyes.

So I lifted him up gently by the hand and as tears welled in my own eyes, I said the words of freedom: "Come with me to the Praetor."

CPSIA information can be obtained at www.ICGtesting.com
Printed in the USA
LVOW11s0908010315

428809LV00001B/54/P